Breathe
Volume VII: The Grudge

Cadillac Press

Cadillac Press
185 Drummond St. Rd
Drummond, NB E3Y 1V9
Canada

Copyright © 2015 Breathe

All rights reserved

Printed in the United States of America

This book, or parts thereof, may not be reproduced in any form without permission. The scanning, uploading, and distribution of this book via the Internet or via any other means without the permission of the publisher is illegal and punishable by law.

Cover image, Old Building 22, by thebitterbullet at deviantart.com

2 4 6 8 10 9 7 5 3 1

FIRST EDITION

Breathe is a network of members, visitors and temporary partakers woven together into a community of writers. We all began in a local area, but since have grown and expanded to all points of the globe.

This is our seventh book together. In it, we sought to tell a story. Each one of us have taken a different character and written through that person's eyes.

Within the pages of this book, you will find all levels of writing, novice to advanced. Some of our group members have been published, some have not. We all seek to share.

Enjoy!

For the love of writing and sharing

AUTHORS

Larry Bubar: Ralph Harper and Frank Bishop
   Larry lives in Presque Isle, Maine. He has been writing for about twenty years. He writes mostly poetry but doesn't consider himself a poet but a writer of humanistic verse for the common folk. He also has written children's books.
   His works include "The Adventures of Frank and Tom (The Ferret Brothers)", "The Rainbow", and books for counting and ABCs for children. He has also written "The Other Side of Midnight" and "Life isn't Always a Bed of Roses" poetry books, as well as partaking in all seven Breath books.

Michelle Lynn Carde: Melony Harper
   Michelle currently lives in Caribou, Maine with her family. Throughout her childhood she involved herself in art and poetry. By the time she reached high school, Michelle had expanded her interest to writing short stories. In late 2005 she began writing her first fantasy novel. In 2010, while attending NMCC for English, Michelle became a member of Breathe, hoping to find help and advice for her work. That same year she was published in Breathe's second book and later was published in Breathe 3, 4, 5 and 6.
   Some of her works include, *To Journey's End*, *The King*, *The Royal Crow*, *Ashwood*, and *Taken*. Hoping to someday publish her work internationally, Michelle continues to surround herself with inspiration to make her dream a reality.

Heather Hunt: Kaori Saint Thomas
   Heather is currently living in Alaska, but her base camp has changed states many times in the past two and a half decades. She has always been a storyteller though it wasn't until her early teens that she relented and began writing the stories down. Since, she has written over a dozen novels though her early efforts might leave something to be desired. In high school and later in

college, she began honing her skill through writing communities and classes.

Her works have graced many online literary magazines and the yearly Breathe Anthology. She is currently working hard at getting more material and learning as much as she can about everything, certain it will be useful somewhere down the line.

Laura Mooney: Beth Avery
Laura is a teacher currently living in New Orleans, Louisianna. She has been part of Breathe throughout all seven books.

Wendy L. Koenig: Hiram Driscoll
Wendy lives in New Brunswick, Canada with her husband, Vince, and their two cats, Jake and Elwood. She is a published author of several books and articles. She is one of the found members of Breathe. Her work can be found at wendylkoenig.com.

Vince Michaud: Randal Snow
Vince lies in New Brunswick, Canada with his wife, Wendy, and their two cats, Jake and Elwood. He graduated from Polyvalente Thomas Albert in 1976. He worked in a warehouse most of his life and he's semi-retired.

Vince is a member of an online writing group where he met his wife. They both meet with the Breathe writer's group in Caribou every week. He has his writing published in eight anthologies.

Breathe VII:
The Grudge

1
The Kidnapper

Hiram Driscoll crept up the carpeted stairs in the pitch black of three AM, Thursday, careful to skip the second and fourth steps. He knew he could tread on the third, but only on the right side. And, though he couldn't see the color in the dark, he also knew the carpet was slate blue.

These things he'd discovered when he'd been in the house yesterday.

In fact, he'd been in the house twice before. His first time, two days ago, he'd come as a city gas man, checking the flow of natural gas coming through the pipes of every house on the block. It was an old ruse, but it always worked. That visit was when he'd first looked inside the house and decided upon and prepared the best entrance for his second trip. And he'd done it right under the nose of the man of the family.

His second visit, yesterday, he'd entered through the kitchen window above the sink. Most people, once they'd locked that particular window, just forgot about it. They put potted plants or some such junk in front of it and never really checked the lock again. He'd come in during the middle of the morning that time, when the kids were at school and Dad was at work. As for the housekeeper, he'd arranged for her mother to have a small accident.

The purpose of this visit was to get the lay of the house. Note its idiosyncrasies. Like the creaking stairs. The nightlight in the hall. Anything he might bump. He didn't need Dad walking into the middle of everything.

Tonight was the final night. The big show. Everything before now had been a dress rehearsal.

He reached the top of the stairs and the nightlight lit his way from there. He eased down the hall to the left, away from the father's room, toward the sanctuaries of the kids. He passed the teenaged boy's room. Barely audible strains and thumps of pop music came through the closed door. It didn't worry Driscoll, though. On his second reconnaissance trip, he'd discovered the kid left the radio on by the unmade bed when not home. He could, therefore, assume the boy left it on even when sleeping.

Driscoll glanced at a giant ornate mirror that seemed to be glowing from the nightlight. Then he stopped and stared. He looked like a stick figure; he'd lost so much weight. When was the last time he'd eaten? His bright orange hair stuck out at odd angles and dark circles underscored his eyes. Maybe he was more of a scarecrow. An evil, demonic one. Yeah. He grinned at his reflection and continued toward the girl's room. He opened her door. The carpet here changed, he remembered. It didn't cause a problem now, but he'd have to remember it on his way out or he'd stumble on the increased thickness. He might even drop the girl.

From where he stood, he saw the pink and yellow butterfly-shaped lights dance across the wall. The girl's room was painted with rainbows and flowers. The floor was carpeted in green, like a field. It had made him smile yesterday, standing beneath the blue ceiling with fluffy white clouds hanging from it.

He wasn't smiling now, though. He reached into his pocket and pulled out the plastic wrapped the towel he'd covered with chloroform. All his attention was focused on the sleeping child as he edged into the room.

A sharp growl erupted from a small ball of fur locked in the girl's tiny arms.

A dog! Well, a puppy. The family didn't have one on either of his earlier visits; he'd checked thoroughly. They had to have gotten it today. Odd that there had been no pet dishes in the kitchen. He frowned, and then spotted the dishes and flattened newspapers on a small tarp, tucked in the corner under a table.

The little growl threatened to explode into a bark. It didn't wake the girl, but it wouldn't take much more before it did. He hated to scrap his plans at the last minute, but it was better than getting caught.

Like nothing was wrong, like he belonged there, Driscoll turned and walked out of the room, through the hall with the nightlight and down the stairs, taking care to skip numbers four and two, stepping only on the right side of step number three.

He let himself out the front door and walked down the block to his car. Everything had been perfect: the night sky was overcast with very little light, the houses in the neighborhood were unlit, even the cops that normally patrolled this area were working a possible burglary downtown. Of course, he'd been the one to smash the jewelry store window for a distraction. It had been perfect.

Then they'd gotten a dog.

He sighed. Even the best laid plans ….

At least he had an alternate plan. He pulled his phone out of his pocket and flipped it open. He'd wake his sister, Emily, but she'd get over it. She always did.

2
The Neighbor

The nightmare had happened again. Randal Snow threw off the covers, sat on the edge of the bed, and jammed his feet into his slippers. His body was soaked in sweat like it always was when he woke from the dream. Randal grabbed his cane by the side of the bed, got up and put on his housecoat. He had little trouble walking anymore; the cane was more for when he stood still. The muscles in his left leg were not strong enough to hold all his weight yet. He went down the hall holding on to the handrail. When Randal walked by the kids' rooms, he checked in on them. Both were sleeping. He made his way to the living room.

The street lamp flowed through the picture window and flooded the floor and coffee table with light. He knew the way to the liquor cabinet without turning on any lamps. Many nights he had found himself here. Randal poured a shot of bourbon and drank it straight down. He often talked when he drank.

"Thank you, Dad," he said as he smacked his lips. He raised his glass in a mock cheer to his father who lived in another state. "You knew I could never afford this bourbon on my own." Then he poured himself a double. He sat in the lazy boy in the dark facing the window. There he had spent most of his rehabilitation years staring out at the world.

Someone passed in front of his window coming from the front of the neighbor's house. Even with the street lamp, all he could see was a person dressed in black, like a walking upright shadow.

"Whoa. Who was that?" Randal blurted out. He got up by the window and saw him disappear down the dark sidewalk. It was strange for the neighbor's teenage boy to be sneaking out of the house. He turned and glanced at the clock on the wall. "It's after three in the morning, I wonder what that boy is doing up so late on a school night. I'm sure it's not an early morning study group. It must be some girl."

Randal shrugged. Finishing his drink, he poured another shot and downed it right away. He walked back to his bedroom as the pain poured out of his body. "Hopefully now, I can get some sleep."

3
The Little Girl

Melony Harper woke to a repeated sharp nibbling and pawing on her nose. Giggling, she gently pushed the young pomsky away, but the anxious pup was determined to keep her awake. Half asleep, she brushed her long, straight, brown hair away from her face and lifted her head to look around the semi-lit room of pink and yellow butterfly-shaped lights.

Beside her, an electronic clock designed after Disney's FROZEN showed that it was just after three in the morning. She flopped her head back onto her pillow and closed her eyes. 6:30 AM would come quickly.

Still near her face, low growls from the pup changed into whines of insecurity as he kept looking over at her open bedroom door. Melony listened, perhaps her father or older brother had gotten up to use the bathroom.

"What's wrong, Frisket?" she asked, becoming agitated.

It had been late yesterday, after school, that they had picked up the newest addition to their family. After months of constantly begging her father for a dog, it just so happened that a neighbor a few houses down from them was giving away six pups to good homes.

Frisket had been the most lively of the bunch. With his blue eyes peeping out from a thick layer of gray and white fur, he was also the best looking. Melony's father had explained that the pup would be nervous for a few days until he had time to adjust to his new surroundings. Scampering to the end of her bed, Frisket jumped off and trotted out of the bedroom.

"Frisket," Melony called in a whisper, but the pup did not return.

Wearing one of her father's old military t-shirts that was two sizes too big and a pair of pink pajama bottoms, Melony climbed out of bed and followed the pup. From her room she could see that Frisket had made it to the staircase and was sniffing the slate blue carpet. Just as she took a step toward him, he disappeared down the stairs.

Hoping her father wasn't still awake, she followed. Passing her older brother's room, she heard music from one of his favorite bands. She wondered how he could sleep with such noise.

"Frisket," she whispered loudly down the stairs.

After waiting a few seconds for the pup to respond, Melony descended into the darkness. With her father's light sleeping, the creaks of the steps would surely wake him.

Feeling for the switch at the foot of the stairs, Melony shed light onto the front entryway where she found the pup sniffing and scratching at the front door.

"There you are," she said, scooping the reluctant pup in her arms. "Daddy will be upset if he finds us down here."

"Mel?" came a deep, groggy voice. Melony turned around to see her father standing at the foot of the stairs wearing a dark blue bathrobe, a white t-shirt, and blue pajama pants. He looked exhausted. "It's late. What are you doing down here?"

"It's Frisket. He's acting weird," Melony replied. "I think he's scared about something."

"We'll figure it out in the morning," he said. "We certainly can't have him keeping you awake all night. Let's get you back to bed. You have school in the morning."

With the pup still tightly in her arms, Melony obeyed her father and ascended the stairs as he went to check the locks on the front door. Returning to her room, she laid the pup beside her and waited for her father to come in.

"Night, Mel," he said, returning a moment later. "Try to get some sleep."

"Night, Daddy," Melony yawned as he tucked her in and headed for the door. "Daddy? Could you close the door, please?"

Her father nodded and quietly shut the door. Melony listened to the sounds of his feet shuffling back to his room. She turned onto her side, wrapped her arms around the pup, and closed her eyes.

There would be no more exploring for Frisket tonight.

4
The Best Friend

Beth Avery — best friend to Melony Harper since kindergarten when Melony managed to escape a kick in the teeth from Beth on the swings — stepped onto the playground after school. Melony was at her side.

"I can't believe you got a puppy!" Beth said. "Can I come see him?"

Melony nodded. "He's so cute!"

Beth pouted a moment. "I want a puppy, too. Mom has her cats. She says that a dog would scare them."

"Cats can be fun."

"Nope. These ones are boring. They're either asleep, outside, or outside sleeping."

The girls walked away from the door, toward the fence, where cars were lined up. Beth leaned onto the metal fence that reached up to elbow-level. "Think of all the things you can do with a puppy! You can run through the park with him, you can teach him to play fetch and do tricks!"

A slap on her back, just above her hanging backpack, shocked Beth out of her daydream. She turned around to see Ryan Starling, running away, laughing. Ryan was a year older, having stayed back a grade, and a head taller than everyone else, and for some reason chose Beth as his favorite victim. His best friend, Peter Hollens, was at his side.

Melony turned to look at the boys, too. She looked away after seeing Peter's glare.

"They're just dumb boys, Mel," Beth said. Even as she said this, though, she knew she hated few things more than bullies, just like her friend did.

The girls were quiet for a few moments. From the corner of her eye, Beth watched the boys leave the playground, and she breathed out a sigh of relief. "Who's picking you up today?"

"Andrew," Melony said, naming her older brother. Her nose curled up a little. Beth felt the same way about her brothers as did Melony. They were just annoying. As soon as she said it, Andrew's car appeared on the side of the street. It was old and green. On the driver's side, there was an orange fender replacing the one that was hit in an accident before Andrew bought it. It was a teen's typical first car.

"Guess that's for me," said Melony. "I'll ask Dad when you can come over to meet Frisket!"

"Great, bye!" Beth leaned on the fence again, her mind drifting. She imagined having a dog, too. Maybe a lab, like her grandparents. She would name it Banjo, for a boy dog, or Heart, for a girl. Beth would take her puppy out for a walk everyday, to get rid of all his energy so he wouldn't bother Mom's cats. She imagined taking him down to Mantle Lake Park, a block from her house. He would chase the geese that flocked to the water and sit with her on a blanket.

"Beth!" This time, it was her Mom's voice that jolted Beth back to reality. "What did I tell you about leaning on the fence, dearest? You're going to get your sweater dirty."

Beth sighed. Convincing her mother to get a puppy would be her goal, now.

5
The Father

Ralph Harper closed his briefcase and left the Houlton District Court. He checked his watch, 3:50 PM. "I should be home in time to get the kids supper," he said to himself. He turned on his cell phone, checked, and saw he had two messages, both from home. He should wait until he got home to find out the "really important news." Instead, he dialed the number. On the second ring his son picked up.

"What's the big emergency today, Andrew."

"Melony is missing," came the reply.

"What do you mean missing?"

"I went to pick her up from school. She wasn't there so I came home but she isn't here either."

"Have you checked her usual places?"

"Yes. I even called Mary's mother to see if she had gone there for a scout meeting. She didn't. I didn't know what else to do, so I called you."

"Okay, I'll be home as soon as I can. Meanwhile think of where she may have gone, or with whom."

"Okay, Dad. Please hurry, I'm really worried."

Ralph hung up, started his car, left the lot, and headed to Presque Isle. At the I-95 off ramp he ran through a red light. He slammed on his breaks, just missing a car turning onto RT 1. He lectured himself, "Pay attention you fool. Pay attention! You don't need an accident at this point in time. Just calm down and watch where you're going."

"Why are you driving so slow? The speed limit is 55. Move it old man!" he yelled at the car in front a moment later. He endured the slow pace of passing through the small towns that were between Houlton and Presque Isle, all the while cursing under his breath. "Only day everyone wants to be on the road."

"Where could she be?" he repeated to himself on the drive home.

Forty minutes later, he pulled into his driveway. He saw Andrew sitting on the porch steps, head in his hands. Ralph got out of the car and started up the walk. Half way to the house, he met Andrew who, upon noticing the car, came running to meet him.

"Okay. From the beginning," said Ralph.

"I got delayed picking up Melony and when I got to her school, she was already gone. I came home and she wasn't here either, so I checked with the neighbors and at the park. When I couldn't find her, I called Mrs. Clow's to see if she was at a scout meeting. She wasn't, so I called you," said Andrew.

"You knew you had to pick her up today because I was in Houlton and Mrs. Melrow has gone to her mother's."

"I know, dad, but I got, uh, er —"

"What was so important you couldn't be there on time?" asked Ralph, anger thick in his voice.

"I, uh, it was a school thing," said Andrew.

Ralph knew by the way Andrew was talking that he was avoiding the question. "Okay, we'll deal with why later. First we have to find Melony. We'll retrace all the places you've checked to make sure she didn't show up after you were there. I'll check the park and drive around the area. You recheck with the neighbors and call Mary again. Also call Beth's, just in case her mother took Melony there since you hadn't shown up."

As Ralph drove around searching for Melony, he couldn't help thinking, 'Too bad the housekeeper's mother had an accident a couple weeks ago, she'd have been at the house and this wouldn't have happened. Hopefully she would be back in a couple weeks. She is the one person I have come to count on since my wife died five years ago. I know I should have gotten a temporary fill-in, but I figured that between Andrew and myself we can hold down the fort until she gets back. At this moment, I guess I figured wrong.'

A half hour later he returned home. Andrew was already there.

"Any luck?" asked Ralph.

"No, you?" replied Andrew.

"No." Ralph went into the house, took his phone list, and made a couple of calls.

"No luck with any of her friends from dance class, either," said Ralph.

"What do we do now?" asked Andrew.

"Only one thing left to do," said Ralph, as he poured himself a glass of whiskey. He took a long pull on the drink and sat down, picked up his phone and dialed.

"Presque Isle Police Department. How may I help you," came a voice from the other end.

Ralph took another swig, "I want to report a missing child."

6
The Reporter

When the unmarked sedan pulled up beside her, Kaori Saint Thomas knew exactly who would be behind the wheel. Doubled-up, hands on her knees, breath misting in the air, and wheezing like the fat kid trying out for football, she was not exactly in the mood to handle the good-natured ribbing that she was certain would commence.

But Detective James Pritchard was her best friend and he never judged her for her obvious character flaws. So she swallowed her pride and her annoyance, took a deep breath that burned all the way down and looked over at him. Sure as sunshine, James was grinning at her from behind the wheel of his police issued sedan.

"Shut...up..." she gasped out.

"You look great, Kaori," he said. She could tell he was trying hard not to laugh but he wasn't trying hard enough. Mirth was redolent in his tone.

She straightened, hand on her side where a stitch had formed. "Next time I decide to quit smoking, remind me of this moment here."

He laughed. "Next time? Don't tell me you've fallen off the wagon."

She twisted her torso, trying to alleviate the persistent ache of the stitch. "No. But I was secretly hoping they were wrong about that whole gaining weight after you quit thing."

"A silly, futile hope. Are you off today?"

She nodded, her bangs plastering themselves to her sweaty cheeks and forehead with the movement. She grimaced and brushed them back. "Only day this week."

"And you use it to go running? You are a glutton for punishment."

"If I wasn't, I wouldn't be working at my ex-husband's newspaper," she said and immediately knew she shouldn't have said anything. She did work for her ex-husband but it wasn't as awkward as one would imagine. However, she knew James thought she should quit and apply for the open position at the Bangor Daily.

"Hop in," James said, mercifully not pursuing the topic of her ex-husband/current boss. James had never approved of Sean, said ex, in any way, shape or form.

She grabbed the handle and let herself in the car, not caring that she was getting sweat on his upholstery. "This is out of character for you," she said, buckling her seat belt. "Also, isn't it against the law for you to drive me home?"

"No. But I can put you in the back if you want. Say I picked you up for vagrancy."

She told him what would happen to his personage if he tried it and he laughed.

"Besides, you're three miles outside of town. Have you considered how you're getting back to your apartment?"

Kaori voiced her thoughts, using several four letter words not suitable for all audiences.

James laughed. "Anyway, I'm off the clock in like ten minutes."

"You just want the Aunts to offer you cookies."

"I can neither confirm nor deny that," he said.

Kaori lived in a basement apartment on Winchester Street. Her landlords were two doddering old ladies who gave her a break on her rent in exchange for help around the house. Kaori, a fan of old movies and plays, sometimes considered the possibility that the aunts were planning to kill her off in some elaborate series of shenanigans.

James thoroughly approved of the Aunts, as Kaori liked to call them. He seemed to think they were a good influence on her.

Kaori could neither confirm nor deny it. She swore less around them and spent more of her time reading than smoking after the Aunts had issued an edict that smoking wasn't allowed inside. Since it was way too cold to do any of that outside, she had gone with the lesser of evils and had quit.

"You want to come in?" Kaori asked as James pulled into her driveway. She opened the door to get out and looked back at him. He probably would have said yes, but his radio squalked.

He reached out to turn it down, frowning as he did so. Kaori found her own lips drawing down.

"No," he said, looking up at her and smiling. Kaori, who knew his smiles better than her own, knew that she had just heard what she thought she had. So, she just nodded, smiled back and got out. She waved as he drove off. She wasn't surprised when he turned right at the stop sign at the end of the street. Right would take him up towards Fleetwood, where the Harper family lived.

She had heard enough of the radio broadcast. She wasn't one hundred percent on her police codes but she knew the code phrase for a missing child.

She stood in her driveway, her heart still pounding from the run, knowing she should go inside, take a hot shower, and maybe write the piece on the McCain's contract. There was a cup of hot tea and some cookies waiting for her.

Instead she pulled her car keys from the pocket of her running shorts, turned on her truck, and pulled out onto Winchester. When she got to the stop sign, she turned right.

7
The Little Girl

"Frisket?"

Melony stood outside her bedroom. The hallway ahead of her appeared like a narrow tunnel that seemed to stretch and disappear into darkness. From beside her, the nightlight took on a reddish glow. Even the slate blue carpet was different. Lighter. Melony peered down to see a scattered trail of dark spots leading away from her. Curious what it could be, she knelt, touching and rubbing the warm wet spots between her fingers. She then touched the substance with the tip of her tongue. From numerous past nosebleeds and losing teeth, Melony was well familiar with the taste of blood. Ew!

"Frisket!"

She called down the hallway again, her voice echoing with fear through the silence. Desperately, she wanted to retreat to her room but felt her body uncontrollably pulling her further through the hallway, away from the safety of the light. Looking behind, her bedroom had disappeared and the light now seemed a mile away. Somewhere ahead of her she heard a faint whimpering and followed its sound.

From out of nowhere, light suddenly appeared and Melony saw what looked to be a man wearing a blue bathrobe. He stood with his back to her, chuckling coldly as his right arm repeatedly moved back and forth very fast in front of him. By now the whimpering had stopped.

"Daddy? Where's Frisket?"

In a flash, the man was now facing Melony, wearing a wide sadistic smile. He was clearly not her father, nor had she ever seen him before. The man held Frisket in one arm while the other held onto a large knife, blood dripping from its tip.

Melony screamed as everything went dark.

Melony woke, her body swaying gently. She slowly opened her eyes to find herself laying on her side, facing what appeared to be the backseat of a vehicle. As groggy as she felt, she just made out the light color fabric of the seat as flashes of yellow from streetlights passed by the back windows.

Andrew didn't have cloth seats. What happened to the leather?

From behind her, loud harsh music blared throughout the vehicle. Andrew never listened to this kind of music. What was going on?

Melony tried lifting her head and a peculiar smell suddenly filled the air, overwhelming her with a wave of nausea and dizziness. It reminded her of rotting food. Feeling sicker, she closed her eyes again and tried lifting her arm to cover her nose, but found herself securely tied.

Why?

Worry filled Melony's mind. She tried to recall the last few minutes when she had first gotten in the car, but her mind felt fogged and disoriented. Even thinking made her weak. She focused harder as pain from a piercing headache began to throb in her temples.

What time was it? Judging by how dark it appeared outside, it had to be evening.

She needed to see what was happening. Melony found turning over onto her left side to be more of a challenge than she had expected. With every movement her pink and white jacket twisted around her body. She tried moving her feet, but found them tied as well. After a few minutes of struggling, Melony at last managed to turn herself. Below her, crumbled bags from various fast food places littered the floor; explaining the strong smell. Andrew never kept his car this dirty. Melony held back from throwing up and focused her attention on the front seat. At this angle she couldn't see the driver, only part of his right arm and side of his head. Panic rose inside her.

She tried calling out, but her words trailed off as blackness overcame her again. Melony concentrated on the loud music that was becoming more and more distant. Eventually, she heard nothing.

8
The Father

Ralph Harper hung up the phone, placed the glass on the end table, and leaned back in his chair. "How long has she been gone? Who saw her last? Where haven't you looked?" These and a hundred more questions were asked by the lady on the phone. Then 'We usually don't deal with missing persons until they've been gone for 24 hours, sir.' What's wrong with the police? My daughter is missing. She's only seven and they want to wait. This is what paying my taxes gets me. Wait until I see the town manager next. I'll let him know what I think." When he told them that Melony was diabetic they said that someone would be sent over.

About fifteen minutes later — though, as far as Ralph was concerned it was an hour or two — a car pulled into his driveway. A somewhat tall, sturdy looking man got out and came to the door. He knocked. When Ralph opened the door, he asked, "Are you Ralph Harper?"

"Yes."

"I'm Detective James Pritchard, from the P. I. Police Department. I'm here in response to the missing person call."

"Come in. This is my son, Andrew," said Ralph, gesturing to the boy sitting on the sofa.

"Who is it that is missing?" Pritchard asked.

"My daughter, Melony. She wasn't at school when my son went to pick her up and hasn't come home, yet."

"When was the last time either of you saw her?"

"This morning, when I dropped her off at school," said Ralph.

"This morning, just before I left for school," said Andrew.

"What about your wife? Was she at home?" asked Pritchard.

"No, she died a few years back. I do have a housekeeper, but her mother was in an accident a couple weeks ago and she went to help out."

"How does Melony usually get home from school?"

"She usually rides the bus or the housekeeper picks her up on days she has scouts or dance class. But, for the time being, Andrew or I have been picking her up."

"Who was to pick her up today?"

"Andrew. I was in Houlton at court. I'm a lawyer," said Ralph.

"Have you looked for her?"

"Of course. We've checked with the neighbors and all the places she might have gone," said Ralph, letting a hint of anger into his voice.

"What time were you supposed to pick her up at school?" asked the detective, looking at Andrew.

"Around three, but I got held up and didn't get there until after 3:25," answered Andrew.

"What does she look like and what was she wearing the last time you saw her?"

Ralph spoke. "She has brown hair, hazel eyes, about three foot nine inches tall and slim built. She was wearing teal jeans, a blue and pink pullover, zebra striped sneakers and socks, and a pink and white spring jacket. She had a pink and white 'Hello Kitty' backpack."

9
The Neighbor

Randal Snow had heard a car pull up in the driveway next door. He'd glanced out the window to see the unmarked police car in Ralph Harper's driveway. He had seen plenty of those cars after the accident, when the detectives would come and question him time and time again. Every new piece of evidence they found carried dozens of new questions. It mattered not to them that Randal had just lost his wife in the accident. Still, three years later, he remembered every last detail of what had happened that night, as if the nightmares he had weren't enough. Randal sat down and it all came back to him.

The night was pitch dark; it was raining and the pavement was like a black mirror reflecting the headlights into the rain. 'Riders On The Storm' from The Doors was playing on the AM radio of the '52 BelAir that he had finished restoring the previous month. The kids were with his parents and Angella and Randal were taking a road trip. They were fifteen miles out of town on a two lane highway when the front wheel pinion on the driver's side broke. The wheel flew out of the fender and the swing arm dug in the pavement, making the car swerve sideways. The car rolled onto its side, its top, its wheels, and its top again, picking up momentum across the road until it crashed in the ditch.

Everything was ejected while it was rolling, including Angella. The only exception: Randal. He was pinned behind the steering wheel. Everything came to a stop, the car laying on the driver's side. He opened his eyes and looked across the seat. Angella wasn't there. Randal lost consciousness. He was told later that the car had rolled over his wife after she had been ejected, killing her instantly.

 He woke from his nightmare memory as something caught the corner of his eye. Someone was outside the Harper's house. Randal got out of his chair to get a better look. The person had disappeared. He dismissed it as kids playing.

10
The Reporter

No one ever locks their garage windows, Kaori Saint Thomas thought as she wiggled her fat hips through the postage-stamp-sized window. She almost got stuck and had to leave her jacket outside. If James saw the jacket, though, she would be in deep trouble. He knew that double breasted London Fog was her favorite coat.

She tumbled gracelessly to the garage floor, barely missing the work bench under the window. She lay on her back for a minute, thanking whoever was in charge of small favors that she hadn't made much noise. Stifling a groan, she got up and dusted off before heading around the car and aiming for the door between the house and the garage.

There was a screen door and then a wood one, inlaid with glass windows. Mercifully there was a curtain over the windows. She inched open the screen door, wincing each time it squawked in protest. When she had it open far enough, she wedged herself between it and the door jamb. She reached for the next door knob, knowing that she was venturing into illegal territory here. If James caught her, there would be no pardon, no looking the other way.

She grabbed the door knob in a hand that was still

surprisingly sweaty for such a brisk spring day. There was a bad moment when the knob didn't turn, but then her luck won through and it slowly opened. She secretly berated Mr. Harper. What kind of person, after your kid disappears, leaves anything unlocked?

She'd parked around the block to keep James from coming out and recognizing her truck and she was worried it had taken her too long to get here, that James and Mr. Harper would be done talking.

She heard James's voice first. "Any other item or distinguishing marks that you think might help us?"

Mr. Harper responded, his voice frayed with concern. "She wears a necklace and bracelet. Both identify her as a diabetic."

"Does she carry her insulin with her?" James again, his voice more sharply pitched. Kaori could imagine the look on his face.

"Usually, I give her a shot before she goes to school. Although she does carry one of those new dial pens for emergencies. All the teachers at school and her friends' moms know about it."

"Okay if I check her room?" James asked and the volume changed, as if he were moving away.

"I guess so," Mr. Harper replied. Kaori could hear the uncertainty in his tone.

"You never know what little thing may pop up somewhere," James said, his voice fading out, accompanied by footsteps as he mounted the stairs.

Kaori realized she couldn't go into the house and continue to eavesdrop. Besides, she'd gotten enough already.

She turned and climbed back out the window. On the other side, she retrieved her jacket and pulled out her cell phone. She punched in Sean's number. Her ex answered on the first ring.

"How is that McCain's piece coming?" he asked in lieu of a greeting.

"What if I had a lead on a missing child case? Possibly a kidnapping?"

There was a long silence. Kaori waited it out. When she heard Sean draw in a breath, she hung up on him. She knew he was going to try to take this from her. He always did. He didn't think she was capable of working on advanced cases like this. She wasn't sure he was wrong, but she wanted the chance to find out herself.

Her phone started ringing again. She silenced it and looked around, wondering where to start. There was a car in the driveway next door. A Cadillac Sedan, in perfect condition. She had never been a car person, but that one made her feel like she could start now.

11
The Father

The detective and Ralph stood in the center of Melony's room. Frisket, who had been curled up in the middle of Melony's bed when they arrived, now circled around the two men's feet, occasionally jumping up on Pritchard's leg.

"Frisket, be good," said Ralph, moving the dog aside with his foot.

"Cute puppy," said Pritchard.

"We just got it yesterday. Melony loves it. That's one reason I can't believe she wouldn't come straight home from school."

Pritchard looked around the room. "Seems like a typical seven year old girl's room. I don't see anything peculiar. Do you have a recent picture of her?"

"Yes. It's downstairs."

Ralph and the detective went back downstairs. Ralph went over to the mantle, above the fireplace, and took down a picture frame.

"This is her latest school picture," said Ralph, handing it to the detective.

"Okay if I take it with me? I'll get it out to local law enforcement and put it up on our Facebook page."

Ralph took the frame, removed the picture and gave it to the detective. "You think it will do any good?"

"You'd be surprised how many people actually check out the site. I'm quite sure it will be of some help. Anyway, it can't hurt."

Detective Pritchard checked his notebook and then placed it in his pocket. "I guess I've got what I need for now. I'll go back to the station and have dispatch let the other officers know and also inform the Sheriff's Department and the State Police, so they can be on the lookout for her. Her being diabetic means the 24-hour waiting period will be waved. If you think of anything that might help us, or if she returns, be sure to let the station know."

"Thanks for coming. I'm sure it's just some mix up, but these days one can't be too careful," said Ralph, trying more to convince himself than the officer.

He stood in the doorway until Pritchard left. Returning to his chair, Ralph picked up his cell phone, scrolled through the phonebook and pushed Frank Bishop's number. It went to voice mail. He said, "This is Ralph Harper. I have a job for you. Please get back to me as soon as possible, no matter what the time. It's very urgent." He then reached for his drink, sat back in his chair, and looked at Andrew. "It's going to be a long, long night."

12
The Kidnapper

Driscoll glanced into his rearview mirror, angling it downward to check on the little girl unconscious on the back seat. He'd heard her stirring, crying out and shifting. Then she'd passed out again. He watched her chest rise and fall with the deep steady rhythm of those who sleep. So far, so good.

He turned his attention back to the road, just in time to keep the car from running off the shoulder, straightening out in his lane, and glancing in his mirrors to see if anyone was around to witness it. Other than the semi way behind him, there was no one else on this stretch of I-95.

His thoughts returned to the girl's father, Harper, and the panic that had been plastered on his face as they'd passed each other on the Houlton Road. What would he be doing at that very moment? Had it dawned on him yet, fully and completely, that his precious daughter had been kidnapped, or was he still searching the city for her, his heart clenched with worry and dread?

On the passenger's seat, under the girl's backpack, his phone buzzed. He didn't like ring tones; they gave away too much information about the phone owner; how he felt about family, friends, or even his outlook on life. No, a buzz was good for him, though it probably said something about his own outlook. His fingers closed on the smooth, flat phone and he fished it out, glancing at the caller ID. Emily.

"Yeah."

"How'd it go?" Her voice was breathless, fast, and a little higher pitched than normal. She was excited.

"Easy as falling out of bed."

"So, really easy, right?"

"Yes. Easy. What good is a simile if you don't trust it?"

"Well, honestly, some of your similes aren't very clear."

"That one was clear."

"That's because you didn't make it up."

Driscoll didn't answer, pouting like a petulant child. The silence stretched between them like the highway he traveled.

After a moment, Emily asked, "So, where are you now?"

"Coming up to Waterville. Traffic on the Houlton Road slowed me down."

"Did you see him?" Again, that breathy voice.

"Oh, yeah. That's one vision I'll never forget." Driscoll smiled at the smooth darkness of the night, the memory of Harper's panic and frustration big in his mind.

"Wish I could have seen it."

"Well, it's your turn, now."

"Revenge feels good, doesn't it?"

"Yes, it does."

Again, there was the silence, but closer, warmer, and friendlier this time. Driscoll came up to the #130 exit into Waterville. He changed lanes, turned on his blinker, and slowed. "She's still sleeping. I'm gonna grab a bite to eat at Mickey Dee's."

"Cover her. We don't want anyone seeing her."

"Ya think? Talk to you when I get closer." Sometimes, Driscoll got really annoyed by Emily; she bossed him like he had no clue. He'd learned from experience that the best thing to do was to just get away from her when she was like that. He closed the phone and set it on the passenger's seat, letting it slide beneath the backpack again. As he pulled into the McDonald's drive-thru, he reached behind him and flipped the old army blanket over the girl. He rolled down his window.

The intercom crackled to life. "Welcome to McDonald's. May I take your order?"

"Yeah. I'll take two Happy Meals."

13
The Father

Friday morning, Ralph Harper sat in his chair, sipping his third cup of coffee. He checked the time, eight AM, he still had a half an hour before he and his friend started their search for Melony. Ralph turned on the TV and clicked on WAGM, for the news. It's volume was turned up, but he wasn't really listening. He was contemplating where to start the search and almost missing a report of a body being found along the bike path in back of the Pine Street School. Immediately, he tried to focus but the report was over before the information could be processed. All Ralph heard was "found body," "burned" and "going to the Medical Examiner in Augusta." He turned off the TV, grabbed his jacket, and headed out the door.

He pulled into the PIPD parking lot between two police cars, got out, and sprinted to the entrance. A young lady sat behind a glass window just inside the lobby. Ralph walked up to it and waited for her to notice him, all the while tapping his fingers on the sill.

"How may I help you?"

"My name is Ralph Harper. Is Detective Pritchard around?" he asked, trying to be calm.

"Yes. He's in the back."

"May I speak with him? It's rather urgent."

"What does it pertain to?"

"It's about my missing daughter," he answered, hearing the frustration building in his voice.

"One moment, please."

The lady picked up a phone. After a few minutes of discussion with someone she hung up.

"Detective Pritchard will be with you in a moment," she said.

Ralph paced back and forth trying to keep from going into crazy mode and doing or saying something he'd regret later. A door in one corner of the lobby opened. Detective Pritchard stepped out.

"Ralph, good to see you. What brings you here?" he asked, extending his hand.

Ralph shook the detective's hand. "I'm here to see if you have any information on the body they found."

"I wasn't called in on that case and the State Police have taken it over, so I don't have much. Come in. Let me see what I can find out."

Ralph followed the detective into the back office.

"Have a seat. I'll make a couple of calls," said Pritchard, motioning to a chair.

Ralph sat down and waited while Detective Pritchard made one call after another. In the end, he had made five.

"What did you find out?" asked Ralph, his impatience showing, not only in his mannerisms, but in his voice.

"Not much. This morning a couple walking on the bike path found a body beside a downed tree."

"Do they know who it was?" asked Ralph.

"It was so badly burned they couldn't make any kind of ID. They do know it was a small person, probably a child. They are still trying to figure how long it's been there."

Ralph's heart skipped three beats. He turned pale and almost fell out of the chair. Detective Pritchard stepped over to where Ralph was sitting and steadied him. "Don't panic yet. There is no evidence that the body was your daughter."

"Doesn't mean it isn't either."

"Let's wait until the Medical Examiner in Augusta can look at it and determine what's what."

Ralph calmed a bit at this suggestion. "Did they find a necklace or bracelet?"

"As far as I know, there was only the body, but they're still processing the area. We won't know anything more until they're done.

"When do you think the examiner will get to it?"

"The body won't get down to Augusta until tonight or tomorrow. So the examination probably won't be until Monday, if they don't have a higher priority case pending."

"That long? I'll be a wreck by then. What case could be a higher priority than this?"

"The Feds could bump anything, even a murder or suspicious death case. I'm sorry there's not much I can do. I'll keep in touch and if I hear anything, one way or the other, I'll let you know."

Ralph stood up and headed out. Detective Pritchard followed him to the main entrance.

"Thank you for the help. Let me know if anything comes up," said Ralph, as he shook the detective's hand and turned to head for his car.

"Will do. And think positive," said Detective Pritchard.

Ralph got in his car and drove home. He went in the house, poured himself a tall glass of whiskey and drank it in one swig. He sat in his chair and stared at the blank T.V.

After a moment, he picked up his cell phone and thumbed through his list until he found Greg Still's phone number. He tapped the call button and waited. The phone rang a million times before Ralph heard a voice mutter, "Hello."

"Is this Greg?"

"Yes it is."

"This is Ralph Harper."

"Oh! Hi, Ralph. How's it going?"

"Not too bad. Yourself?"

"Okay! What can I do for you?"

"Are you still working with the Medical Examiner's Office?"

this?"

He gave her a look but nodded. "Might as well."

She set up the record app on her phone and hit the button to start it. "Was there anything out of the ordinary yesterday morning with Melony?"

"No," he said. "As you know, she has diabetes. She has to go to the nurse at lunch to do her test and sometimes we have to administer insulin. Usually she is good about it or else her father handles it."

"No problems there, then," she said.

"Nothing at all during the day. Her brother goes to the high school, and lately he's been picking her up. Her teacher knows her brother."

"Then, how did Melony wander off?"

Henry was silent for a long moment and Kaori wondered if she had pushed her luck enough. She was about to excuse herself when he spoke again.

"Her teacher says she got into her brother's car."

It was Kaori's turn to fall silent. She remembered the note of panic in the brother's voice. Had it been his car or just a car that looked like his? Either way, it changed the story. Melony didn't wander away from school. She had either been taken or she had disappeared from a different location. Had her brother stopped somewhere on the way home? Had Melony gotten out and been left or...

Kaori turned off her phone. "Okay. I need to look into this. Thanks, Henry."

He started to rise then sat back down and reached into his drawer for a pen. He pulled a pad of Post-Its over to him and scribbled a note.

"This is her teacher's information," he said, tearing it off and handing it over. He scribbled again. "And this is Mike Douglas. He's her brother's best friend. He's home today on suspension. I don't know if you'll find out anything. I don't even know what's going on, but hopefully you won't run into a dead end. Melony is a sweet girl. We want her safe."

Kaori took both notes and got to her feet, shoving the papers into her jacket pocket with her phone. "Thanks, Henry. I owe you one."

"I'll expect that to carry through next time we do a fundraiser. I'll be expecting a nice article," he said. His tone was jovial but she could see that he was just as worried about the missing girl as her father was.

On a hunch, Kaori went to the teacher's room. Some of the doors in the hallway were closed, in session. A few were open, empty of students. She found the room she wanted, happy it was one of the latter classrooms, knocked on the open door, and stepped in.

The teacher, Ms. Ouelette looked up from where she sat at her desk. There was a haunted look in her eyes and Kaori understood.

"Can I help you?"

"I'm hoping you can. You're Melony Harper's teacher, right?"

Kaori saw her face go hard and put her hands up hastily. "I'm not looking to blow this out of porportion. I just...I just want to know what happened."

"I'm sure you do," the teacher said. "But the last thing that family or this school needs is some glory hound reporter trying to make a name for herself."

"I'm not —" Kaori began.

"Get out of my classroom."

"But Henry —" Kaori tried again.

"I said, get out."

Kaori backed out and found the door shut in her face none too gently. She pursed her lips but decided to let it go. She shrugged into her jacket and fumbled out her keys. Halfway to her car something occurred to her.

"Crap," she muttered. "I hope I'm wrong."

15
The Little Girl

"Melony?" A man's voice faintly echoed through Melony's mind.

"She doesn't look good." A second voice echoed the first. This time it was a woman's.

Melony partially opened her eyes to see two blurred figures standing closely in front of her, one pacing behind the other, its movement causing a wave of nausea. Melony closed her eyes to prevent herself from vomiting. Her body felt weak and fatigued. Even lifting her head seemed like a struggle.

The voices continued.

"I found this in her backpack," the woman said quietly.

"Let's wait to use it until absolutely necessary," replied the man. His voice certainly wasn't her father's. "I think she's just groggy from the chloroform."

Melony's mind felt like a blank canvas. She tried to remember what had happened, but instead only caught flashes of a disturbing dream. The man must have noticed her strained look. She felt a rough hand touch her cheek. Melony opened her eyes again as colors of bright orange from the man's figure moved in and out of her vision.

"Melony? Can you hear me?"

Melony hesitated, then slowly nodded. She ordered her mind to stay awake, listening to the voices that continued to converse back and forth. The blurred figure of the woman walked away and disappeared from view. The air felt cold, like someone had left a front door open. A peculiar yet familiar smell filled Melony's nose. It reminded her of the ocean in some ways, like when her family had taken trips to the coast of Maine. Where was she?

"Melony," the man's soft voice brought her attention back to him. "My name is Driscoll."

Melony's vision sharpened and gradually became clear. She focused on the man's face more closely. Freckles dotted his cheeks, nose, forehead, and around his green eyes. His bright orange hair stuck out at different angles, reminding her of the man from her nightmare. Could he have been the same one? Fear started to come back to Melony as tears formed around the edges of her eyes.

"We found this in your backpack," he continued. Melony watched as he pulled from his back pant pocket her GlucaPen. "You're diabetic. Are you type one or two, Melony?"

"One," Melony choked back tears.

Driscoll looked it over once and returned it to his pocket.

"And here I was thinking this would be easy." He ran his hands through his hair.

Melony was unsure if he was saying this to her or to himself.

"Where am I? Where's my daddy? What did you do with Frisket?" She sobbed, her voice sounding panicked even to her own ears.

"Don't be afraid. I promise you're safe," Driscoll continued. "Here. I got you a Happy Meal. You like these? It's probably cold by now, but I figured you'd be hungry when you woke."

Melony looked at the food in front of her and felt her stomach growl despite her nausea. She couldn't remember when she had last eaten nor how long she had been asleep. Both hunger and thirst overwhelmed her. Attempting to reach for the food, she suddenly realized her hands and feet were tightly tied to a chair. Driscoll chuckled at this.

"Forgive me. I almost forgot."

Untying her hands, he kept her feet secured and handed her the Happy Meal. "As weak as you are, I don't think I have to worry about you getting very far. Eat. You'll feel better."

Melony watched as Driscoll stood up and limped towards a metal door behind him, noticing his left leg was twisted inward. Sliding the door open, he looked back at her with a grin and closed the door.

Wiping her tears on the sleeve of her coat, she looked around the semi-lit room. Three low hanging lamps shed light on some boxes and crates that lined the corners of the walls. The floor below her was made of concrete. Beside a pile of crates, was an air vent where, most likely, the cold air was coming from.

From outside, she heard Driscoll talking to the woman, but couldn't make out any words. The woman's voice sounded harsh, but died down and, in a few minutes, the door slid open again. Melony stopped eating, her eyes focused on the woman as she entered.

"Hi, Melony," the woman spoke kind and softly. A smile was spread across her face as she approached and knelt down before Melony. She looked tired. Dark circles underscored her eyes. "You have such a beautiful name. My name is Emily. I can tell you and I are going to be great friends."

16
The Reporter

Kaori was not wrong when she left the school at ten AM. As she pulled into the Douglas' driveway, she saw Mrs. Douglas peek through the curtains at her, cellphone glued to her ear.

Kaori sighed but killed the engine and got out of her truck. She knew what the result would be of this little adventure but she had to try it anyway.

To her surprise, it was Mr. Douglas who opened the door. He was surprisingly young looking for a man in his early fifties. In fact, he looked a little like a young Marlon Brando.

"Can I help you?" he asked.

"Don't let her in!" shrilled a female voice from the left.

Mr. Douglas did not even flinch. "You're Kaori Saint Thomas, right?"

Kaori opened her mouth to confirm when the woman shrieked again. "I've been on the phone with Ms. Ouellette and if you let her in that door, Charles, I swear I'll divorce you," the woman yelped like a ...

"Shut up, you harpy," Mr. Douglas replied, his voice never raising above a dull roar.

… Harpy, Kaori thought. That was the word she'd been looking for.

"What can I do for you?" Mr. Douglas asked.

"I was hoping to speak with Mike."

He nodded. "That's fine."

"WHAT!" his wife shrieked behind him.

"You realize it will be Mike's decision if he tells you anything or not," Mr. Douglas pointed out. "And Woman, shut up!" This last was directed over his shoulder. He looked back at Kaori. "His room is upstairs on the left."

He stepped back to let her in. Kaori heard footsteps and a door slammed somewhere in the house.

"You aren't going to get in trouble?" Kaori asked. "With your wife, I mean?"

Mr. Douglas shrugged. "I'm always in trouble. These things blow over fast with her."

Kaori wasn't sure how to respond to that so she just nodded. She stepped past him. The foyer led straight to the stairs and she climbed them, trying to sort out her questions in her mind as she did. She didn't usually do things like this, fly-by-the-seat-of-her-pants investigations. Usually she was meticulous and exacting and had every question phrased perfectly to elicit the answers she wanted.

But this was exciting. She didn't read mysteries; was more of a horror fan. She had no idea if she was doing any of this right but she knew she had to try.

She hesitated, then knocked on the door. There was a pause and a teenager opened the door. She supposed he looked normal, or at least whatever passed for normal in teenagers these days. His mousy brown hair was spiked and he had several piercings in each ear. He wore a Breaking Benjamin tee shirt and jeans that seemed barely able to stay on his hips. The only thing out of context were the Buddy Holly glasses perched on his nose.

"Hey," he said, opening the door wider and pushing the glasses up his nose. She got a glimpse of his room; dirty clothes piled haphazardly around, Japanese manga magazines scattered across the bed. There was a desk with the remnants of homework and a half eaten sandwich that looked like it had tried to slither off the plate before succumbing to rigor mortis. Beside all of that, she recognized the bottle of contact lens solution.

"You're that reporter lady, right?" he asked. "You covered the snow sculpture contest we had back in January."

He didn't mention that it was a fluff piece, but he didn't have to. Kaori had never taken an overly abundant amount of pride in her work as a journalist, but she did like the occasional fluff piece.

"I was hoping to talk to you about Melony and Andrew," she said.

He blinked behind his glasses, then stepped back. "Uh, yeah. Okay. Come in."

She stepped into the room, minding her feet. She was wearing her running shoes still, but she felt like she should be wearing a full Hazmat suit in there.

"Tell me about Andrew and his sister," she asked, leaning a hip against his desk.

"What's to tell?" Mike asked, flopping onto the bed. He reached under him and pulled out a tennis shoe and tossed it into the corner of the room. He didn't seem to notice the cloud of dust that rose from the shoe landing.

"Do they get along?"

"Yeah, well enough, I guess. Mel's a bit of a clinger. Andrew calls her The Barnacle." Mike chuckled.

"And lately, Andrew has been picking up Melony after school?"

"Oh, yeah. There's this group of college girls that volunteer at Mel's school and Andrew likes to impress."

"So what happened today?"

Mike shrugged. "Dunno. I usually hitch a ride and we go to his place and play video games, but Andrew said he had other plans."

"And he didn't say what plans?" she asked.

"Didn't say. Didn't ask."

17
The Kidnapper

Midmorning, Driscoll rifled through the kid's backpack, shoving books and odd-shaped zipper cases out of the way, searching for the one thing he needed. As he searched, his movements became more erratic. Finally, his teeth gritted and bared like a rabid dog, he dumped the backpack upside down, strewing its contents across the ancient card table that predominated the dusty room.

With a feral, choking cry, he snatched up the boy's black cell phone that slid out last from a side pocket. Driscoll had dropped it in the backpack to put his phone call out of his mind, to keep him from making it too early. But, now it was time.

He rubbed his thumb back and forth across its smooth surface, remembering how Harper took his son away by getting a court injunction so that he couldn't see his boy ever again. It burned inside him every second of every day. Everything he and Emily did came to revenge for what Harper had done.

He stood and slipped it into the front pocket of his jeans. After checking that the kid's room was locked tight, Driscoll wedged the exterior door to the building open wide enough for him to shimmy through. Leaving the door open, he climbed into his ancient Impala, grinning at the menacing, throaty roar it gave when he started it. Emily appeared at the warehouse door. Her face wore its perpetual grimace as it did when she had to be near children. When she nodded at him, he drove off.

He took the first right, toward the waterfront, then two lefts. At the next intersection, he drove up the highway access road and pulled onto I-95 North, the phone in his pocket burning its presence into his mind.

18
The Father

Ralph looked at his watch, 11:30 AM. He'd been on the road since a little after nine. Augusta was probably another two and a half or three hours away. He figured he should get to the Medical Examiner's office before they quit for the day. Greg had called in a few favors but finally the ME agreed to start on the body as soon as it arrived. Around 1:45 PM, Ralph pulled into the ME parking lot. He took a sip of the cold coffee he had gotten in Bangor, dumped the rest, and went into the building.

A receptionist was just hanging up the phone when he got to her desk. She smiled at him. "May I help you?"

"I'm Ralph Harper and I'm here to see Greg Still. He's expecting me."

"One moment, please." She picked up the phone and pressed a button. After a few seconds, she spoke into the handset. "Mr. Ralph Harper is here."

When she hung up, she said, "Mr. Still will be right with you. Please, have a seat."

Before he'd even found a magazine, Greg, a short, stout man about Ralph's age approached with tall lanky man with grayish hair. Greg said, "Hi, Ralph. Good to see you again," "Though, I wish it was under better circumstances."

Greg turned to the man with him. "Dr. Gran, I'd like you to meet Ralph Harper. He's an ex-Navy JAG I roomed with on an aircraft carrier during a Mediterranean deployment. We're also in the same reserve unit."

"Good to meet you. I'm assume you're the reason I'm pushing this case ahead of the line?" said the doctor, as he extended his hand.

"I'm afraid you're right about that," said Ralph, shaking the doctor's hand.

"Doc, would it be all right if Ralph was in the room when we do the exam?" said Greg.

"Afraid not. It would compromise any evidence we got and may even call into question any evidence there from other cases."

"I didn't think so, but I gave it a shot. Ralph, guess you'll have to stay here in the lobby or maybe go get something to eat," said Greg.

"I'll wait here," said Ralph.

Greg showed Ralph a place he could hang out while waiting. He retrieved a tube, removed a swab, and asked Ralph to open his mouth.

"If nothing else provides a clear answer, we'll do a DNA test. We can't do it until Monday and it may take a day or so to get an answer," said Greg.

"I hope it doesn't come to that. I'll go nuts in that amount of time," said Ralph.

Greg took the sample, placed the swab back in the tube, and then went into the exam lab. Ralph decided on an old <u>Time</u> magazine and took a seat. He tried his best to concentrate on the articles but found himself looking at his watch about every fifteen minutes and wondering what was taking them so long. He even tried going outside and walking around, but this did little to calm him so he returned to the lobby, sat and waited. It was almost two hours before Greg came out from the lab. Ralph immediately jumped to his feet, covering the distance between them in two steps.

"What did you find out?" Ralph asked, fear in both his voice.

"Sorry it took so long. Dr. Gran wanted to complete the autopsy before I spoke to you. It's not your daughter. Although tests proved the body had been burned within the last couple days, the bone brittleness suggests that the body is old. Also, Dr. Gran says the bone structure is that of an Asian or Native American child, not a Caucasian. And, if that wasn't enough, we found this," Greg held out his hand and showed Ralph a tiny, pointed flint object. "Dr. Quell believes it is what's left of an arrowhead. It was embedded in the rib cage of the body. So it's probably a few decades old, but we'll have to do further tests to find out. Right now, we're guessing someone dug up a body from some grave site someplace, burned it and then dumped it where it was found. We're still at a loss as to why. But, you can rest assured that the body isn't your daughter's."

"I'm so relieved. I can't thank you enough for everything you people have done. Please let Dr. Gran know how grateful I am. I need to head back home. Andrew is there by himself and I don't want to leave him for too long. I owe you one, buddy," said Ralph.

"You bet you do, and a big one at that. Fear not, I will collect on it one day. Now, if you'll excuse me, I have a couple phone calls to make to various police agencies," said Greg.

Greg headed toward the office. Ralph gathered his coat and went out to his car. Minutes later, he was back on the interstate headed home. He dialed Andrew's phone, no answer. After several rings he hung up and dialed the home phone.

"Hey Dad, what's going on? You were gone when I got back from school."

"Why didn't you answer when I dialed your cell?"

"I must have left it in my car, sorry. What do you need?"

"Good news! The burned body they found wasn't Melony's. I'm on my way home now. Should be there in a few hours. Can you handle your supper okay?"

"Yep, I got the money you left. See you when you get home. And great news on the body not being Melony."

Ralph hung up his phone. Immediately, it rang.

19
The Kidnapper

Hiram Driscoll had traveled three and a half hours until he reached Bangor, Maine, and turned onto Maine State Route 9. Driving a little over two more hours had brought him to U.S. Route 1, which led to the Maine-Canadian border. In the U.S. border city of Calais, he pulled into the McDonald's on North Street and parked.

Driscoll's breath came in short, rapid bursts now, the adrenalin fueling his body. He felt like he was on a tequila high. His fingers shook as he pulled the boy's phone out of his pocket, so much so that he nearly dropped it twice while dialing the number committed to his memory. Every phone number, every address, every email that Harper had, he knew. He wrapped a small piece of plastic and a red bandana around the bottom of the phone, covering the microphone, but leaving the speaker free.

Harper answered, "Andrew, I thought you left your phone at school?"

Driscoll's mouth dried. For a moment, he just listened to Harper's presence on the other end of the connection. He wished he could see the man's face, his anguish when he heard the threats. He shrugged. This would have to do. Dropping his voice to a low breathy growl, he spoke through the bandana and the plastic. "Do you know who this is?"

It took only a split-second before Harper answered, his voice sharp, angry, but also desperate and destroyed. "You better not hurt my daughter."

In spite of himself, Driscoll laughed. It was no easy feat to do and keep his voice altered. This moment felt so delicious, he wanted to stay in it forever. Sobering, he said, "It's never a good idea to threaten the man who holds life and death in his hands, JAG. Do you think that the similarity of that burnt body to that of your daughter was just a coincidence? If you screw me around, it'll be her next time. I want $250,000. It'll make the pain of losing my boy livable. You have eighteen hours. I'll call you with details at that time."

He hung up and tossed the phone into a trash receptacle as he drove out of the parking lot. Turning west again, he began the long drive back to Boston, grinning from ear to ear, and humming a Karen Carpenter song about being on top of the world. His only regret was that Emily hadn't been there to hear how well he'd done.

20
The Best Friend

"You know, Mom," Beth said Friday night. She left her pigtails in purposefully when she got home from school today, knowing that would impress her mother. They bounced on her shoulders every time she walked and she had to refrain herself from pulling them out. "Melony got a dog the other day."

Mrs. Avery pursed her lips. "Just because Melony got a dog doesn't mean you're going to, Beth." She turned away from her daughter and began unloading the dishwasher.

"But Mom! I would do everything for it!"

Her mother sighed. "Beth, we will have this conversation when you are older. For now, I do not want to hear anymore about it."

Beth opened her mouth to protest again, but before she could get words out, the doorbell rang and Mrs. Avery went to answer it. Beth could hear a man's voice talking and peeked around the corner to see who it was.

The man standing in the doorway was tall and had light brown hair. Beth had never seen him before. She gasped a little when he held up a gold police badge.

Mrs. Avery went over to Beth, placed her arm around her. "Beth, please go into the kitchen for a moment. I need to talk with the nice policeman." She led her into the other room. Beth could feel her heart racing. Why did Mommy need to talk with a policeman? It could be something exciting. When she tried to listen against the door, she could only make out whispered words and gasps. A few minutes later, her mother retrieved her back to the living room sofa.

"Beth," Mrs. Avery said, "the policeman has some questions for you, dearest. But don't worry, you're not in trouble. Mommy will be here the whole time."

Beth felt her breath catch. What could be so important that the policeman would need to talk with her about? What was going on?

"Hello, Beth, my name is Detective Pritchard. I need to ask you a few questions about your friend, Melony."

"What's wrong with her?"

"Beth, she's missing. Her brother was supposed to pick her up from school yesterday, but she was gone by the time he got there. No one has seen her since yesterday after school."

Beth's eyes and mouth became wide holes filled with her panic.

"Most of the time when kids go missing, it's just a mix-up, a miscommunication. Maybe a friend or relative thought they were supposed to pick Melony up when it was her brother's day to do so. But, just in case, I need you to tell me about yesterday afternoon. Can you help me, Beth?"

The little girl nodded. She nervously twisted one pigtail end around her finger.

"Were you with Melony yesterday after school?"

"Yeah--yes. W-we got out of school...and...were waiting by the f-fence to go h-home."

Mrs. Avery moved closer to her daughter. "Dearest, remember that the detective wants to help Melony. It will be okay."

Detective Pritchard continued. "Did anybody talk with you or Melony?"

Beth shook her head. "No. We were talking together until her r-ride came." Her eyes were filled with tears. They were basins of her fear.

"Melony got into the car before you left?"

Beth nodded.

"All right. Now, Beth, this next question is very important. I need you to describe exactly what the car looked like. Can you do that for me?"

"It looked...like Andrew's car! That's why Melony got inside of it!" Beth brushed the tears away with the back of her hand.

"I know, Beth. What color was the car?"

"It's g-green," she said between sobs.

Mrs. Avery stood up to reach Beth some tissues.

"Was there anything remarkable about the car? Bumps, scratches, things like that?"

Beth used the tissue to blow her nose and then frowned. "Andrew's car has an orange part on its side. But...I c-couldn't see it on th-this car. Wrong side."

The detective noted this down on a little pad of paper. "You've done very well, Beth. I have just one more question for you. Could you see who was driving the car?"

"No. I-I didn't look!" Beth's tears fell hard, leaving her eyes red and her nose raw. Her mother buried the little girl into her ample shoulder.

The detective stood up and said that Beth did very well with remembering and this information would help Melony. He was sure it was all a misunderstanding, anyhow.

Beth hardly heard his words of reassurance. The sobs of her grief were deafening.

21
The Neighbor

There came a knock at the door. Randal Snow wasn't expecting anybody. Both kids were in their rooms and it was almost bedtime for them. He grabbed his cane and hobbled to the front door to see who it was. He hadn't heard a car pull up in his drive. That gave him the notion that it might be some sort of door to door salesman, or worse yet, a Bible pusher. He got to the door and looked through the peephole. It was the detective from the unmarked police car he saw earlier at Harper's house the day before. Wondering why he was standing there, Randal opened the door.

"Hello. What can I do for you?"

"Hello, I'm Detective Pritchard from the PIPD. Do you mind if I ask you a few questions?"

"Yes, I do mind. Get off my property."

"Did I say something wrong? Is it a bad time?"

"The accident has been over for three years. I'm done answering questions."

"Sir, this isn't about any accident. Can I come in?"

He grudgingly let the detective inside and led him to the kitchen where he pointed out a chair with his cane. The officer sat down and Randal took the chair across from him. The detective had brought a zippered organizer, which he slowly opened and took out a file folder.

"So, what's this about?" asked Randal.

"It's a missing child investigation." He took out a picture of Melony and put it on the table. "Have you seen this little girl today?" asked Detective Pritchard.

"That's the Harper girl next door, Melony. When did she go missing?"

"She didn't come home from school yesterday."

"Really? I was at school picking up my kids and I was parked two cars behind his son's car. I saw her get in."

"Are you sure it was yesterday?"

"Of course I'm sure. He drives a compact car, green with an orange fender. It's right there in their yard."

"Did you see anybody else come to the car?" Detective Pritchard asked, while writing down notes on his legal pad.

"As soon as the little girl got in the car, they left. Then my kids arrived."

"I wonder if your kids saw anything?"

"They didn't," Randal promptly added.

"How can you be so sure?" Detective Pritchard asked.

"I've told my kids not to fraternize with the Harpers next door."

"Why is that, may I ask?"

"He represented the insurance company when I had my accident that killed my wife. He was pushing for vehicular manslaughter. It was in a car that I had restored, a '52 Chevy BelAir."

"I'm sorry for your loss. I'm sure he was only doing his job."

"I don't think so. It got real personal. My whole life and that of my family was splashed over the evening news and in all the papers for two whole years."

"I'm sorry about that." The detective looked uncomfortable and didn't speak.

"Yes, well, the wounds are deep and still fresh. He did everything he could to discredit me." Randal was starting to get wound up.

"Could we come back to the reason why I'm here?"

"Sorry, I didn't mean to burden you with that. You didn't write any of that down, did you?" Randal stretched his neck to look at the legal pad.

"No, I didn't. Did you notice anything out of the ordinary at the Harper house or in the neighborhood?"

"As a matter of a fact, I did. The night before, or should I say early yesterday morning? I saw the neighbor boy walk through the driveway and down the sidewalk at three AM."

"May I ask what you were doing up at that time?"

"Not at all. I had a nightmare and woke up to get a drink of water."

Pritchard looked at the layout of the house. "From which window did you spot the neighbor boy?"

"It was from that window." Randal pointed with his cane to the window in the living room. "I was sitting in the recliner."

"Are you sure it was Andrew Harper? Did you see his face?"

"I didn't see a face. He was wearing a black hoodie and black pants, and it looked like he stepped right out of the house."

"Where were you when you saw this?" asked the detective.

"Right in this chair. Sit, and you'll see."

Detective Pritchard sat in the recliner and looked out the window. "I see what you mean. He would've come off the front porch, down the driveway and up the sidewalk. How far away did you see him walk? Why didn't he use his car?" Detective Pritchard stood and walked to the window.

"I was at that window by the time he had reached the sidewalk and watched him walk into the darkness. Beats me why he didn't use his car. Maybe he didn't want to wake his father. He could have been meeting someone down the block."

"I didn't mean for you to answer that last question. I was speculating. Thank you for your time, Mister Snow. You've been a big help. Can you make yourself available if I have anymore questions?" Detective Pritchard got up and extended his hand to Randal.

"Sure. Glad I could help." Randal got up and shook hands with the detective and walked him to the door. "I feel bad for the little girl, if there's anything else I can do..." he let his voice trail off.

"I appreciate that. Goodbye, Mister Snow." Detective Pritchard opened the door.

"Goodbye, Detective." Randal waited until the detective walked clear of the driveway then shut the door.

22
The Reporter

When Kaori got home late Friday, she found a note from the Aunts taped to the microwave in her basement apartment. Usually the Aunts never ventured down into her dungeon-esque place of lodging but when she read the note, she saw why they had this time.

Kaori- We're headed to Bar Harbor for the week to see our niece. She's having trouble with her divorce. We should be back by next Friday. Help yourself to the kitchen. Water the plants on Thursday.

Below there was a post script, scribbled by the elder Aunt, whose writing was atrocious. It took Kaori a moment to read it fully.

James came by. Wants to talk to you.

Kaori made a face. That could not be good. She pulled out her cell and saw she had a missed call from him. She checked the time stamp and saw he had called while she was talking to some of Melony's friends. That figured.

When people were stressed, they coped with it in different ways. Until recently, Kaori had always smoked a cigarette. She thought about it, then looked at the digital readout from the outdoor thermometer. It was already in the low thirties.

She sighed and pulled out a can of soup from the cabinets. The cabinets were looking bare. She needed to go grocery shopping today if she wanted to eat through the week. As she started the soup on the stove, she glanced at the calendar she'd taped to the fridge. Tomorrow was Saturday and she had no events to cover until Wednesday. She'd have to do some background work for her article on Tuesday, but she could do that in twenty minutes down at the library. She knew the place like the back of her hand.

So what to do? She chewed on a thumbnail as she contemplated the thought. The smart thing would be to avoid any place James might be. If she poked her nose in too often, he would get suspicious.

On the other hand, there was the theory of hiding in plain sight. If she deliberately avoided him, he would *know* something was up. She usually made time at least twice a week to hang out with him. Perhaps a token appearance was in order.

The soup boiled over. With a muttered curse, she turned off the stove and drew out a bowl.

23
The Little Girl

The next morning, Melony wrapped her pink and white jacket tightly around herself, shivering from the cold drafts that blew in through the small air vent in the storage room. She missed Frisket terribly. Had anyone had remembered to feed and take care of him during her absence? She wondered if help would even come. Would she see her family again? Would they find her before...?

From somewhere outside Melony's imprisonment came an argument of voices, bringing her back to the horrifying reality that surrounded her. She strained to listen.

Allowed freedom from the chair she had been tied to hours ago, she followed the sounds along the sides of the storage room to where the small air vent near the bottom of the wall left, of the room's only door.

Not knowing how it was done, Melony had tried picking the lock of the door many times with her hair clips, but neither Driscoll nor Emily was never too far away from constantly checking in on her. This barely gave her any time to find a way to escape.

Getting down on her hands and knees, Melony listened. Driscoll and Emily could be heard arguing back and forth.

"Have you lost it?! This wasn't part of the plan," Emily shouted, her voice sounding loudly through the vent.

"It's been part of the plan since the beginning," Driscoll's voice replied. "I didn't feel it was necessary to tell you. You forget, I give the orders here! Your job was only to keep the girl calm and preoccupied. That's it. Not to run the entire operation!"

"I can see why the military kicked you out. Harper did you a favor. Apparently you've learned nothing with that narrow-minded, egotistical, pathetically warped brain of yours. You're supposed to kill the enemy, you idiot. Not keep her as a pet!"

"The girl is not the enemy!" Driscoll screamed, making Melony jump back a few inches from the vent.

For a moment, there was silence. Then, Emily's voice was heard again, her tone becoming much harsher, even menacing. "She's the daughter of your enemy. That makes her one, too. The girl must die!"

At this Melony gasped and scurried to the only shelter in the room, where she huddled with her back against the chair. She rocked herself back and forth as tears streamed down her cheeks. "Daddy..." she silently cried over and over.

Nausea and sickness overwhelmed her once more. She couldn't remember when she had eaten the McDonald's Happy Meal, nor when she had been given her GlucaPen. Her body felt so weak and tired. Her fear and anxiety only increased her symptoms.

Did she really just hear what she heard? Or could she be becoming delusional?

Melony knew she needed to find a way out soon and get help. It was her only chance. She didn't know which would be worse, being killed by Emily or by her illness.

24
The Reporter

After a quick shower Saturday morning, Kaori raided the Aunt's kitchen. As she had suspected, there were no less than three tins of newly baked cookies. The Aunts seemed to think a person could survive on cookies alone. Sometimes Kaori thought they were on to something, especially after she had a particularly nasty argument with Sean.

Today, she would not be using the cookies to alleviate her self loathing. Today, the baked goods would have a different purpose.

She pulled out an empty tin and filled it, putting in primarily gingersnaps, which were James's favorites.

The Presque Isle Police Department did not look like there was a crisis going on. Kaori expected a tip line ringing off the hook, patrolmen and women bustling around, white boards filled with copious notes. When she got in, it was anything but the bustling image she had garnered from TV and movies. In fact, the squad room was desolate, full of empty desks. With one exception.

Daphne Williams, one of the patrolwomen was sitting at her desk, her fingers flying over her keyboard as she worked on a report or something like it. She looked up. "James isn't in. He probably won't be in all morning."

Her hands never stopped moving on the keyboard but Kaori had learned not to take it personally. Daphne was one of those rare individuals who could work on two things at once and neglect neither.

"The k-uh, missing girl?" Kaori had almost said kidnapping before remembering that it wasn't confirmed yet. She knew that the police hated it when citizens jumped to conclusions like that. James had a full tangent on it that he launched from time to time on their movie nights.

"Yeah," Daphne said, freeing one hand to grab her coffee. She took a swig and winced. Kaori set her own coffee on Daphne's desk. "Help yourself."

Daphne took a sniff. "Pumpkin spice? Thought they stopped this back in the fall."

"Home brewed," Kaori said. "So what is James up to today?"

"Supervising the protective detail on Hans Vernon."

The name was familiar but it took Kaori a moment to place it. "Wait, isn't that the sex offender that moved in back in August? Out on Chapman Road?"

Daphne drained Kaori's coffee and handed it back to her. "Thanks. I needed that. I'm surprised you remember Vernon. Public memory is usually pretty short for these kinds of things. Not to mention almost no one reads the bulletins we send out."

"Was he a pedophile?" Kaori asked, starting to connect the dots.

Daphne nodded, back to typing. "The girl in question was thirteen and looked like she was sixteen but no one seems to care about that."

"So, are we looking at a mob here?" Kaori asked.

Daphne looked at her, hands stilling as she devoted her full attention to Kaori. "Let's just say it'd be best if that little girl shows up soon and in good health."

Kaori felt a shiver run down her back. "So, any chance you'd tell me the address?"

Daphne went back to typing. "You know I won't."

Her choice of words – won't as opposed to can't – was not

lost on Kaori, who made her living from words.

"Fair enough," Kaori said. "I just came by to drop off cookies anyway. Mind if I put them on James's desk?"

"No snooping," Daphne said.

"Got it," Kaori said, which was not exactly a promise. Luckily, Daphne was back into her work and seemed not in the mood to argue semantics. Kaori slipped past her and into the back section of the squad room, where the detectives' desks were. There were only two detectives, James and Eric Stevens, an older man who mostly worked with narcotics cases. She set the cookies down and glanced over James's desk. His computer was useless. He only used it for closed cases.

Instead she took out her phone and took a few quick pictures of the sketchbook he kept beside his computer. Unlike most people, James preferred the unstructured format the sketchpad offered him and used it for notes to himself.

She pocketed her phone and left, waving to Daphne as she did so.

In her truck, it took Kaori a little less than twenty minutes to figure out James's note system. She'd had much experience with his notes. He usually started in one corner then merged to take over the rest of the page. The smaller the note, the later it was written. At least, it generally meant that. She used her phone's internet to search for names, doing her best to decipher James's writing. His writing was remarkably neat and legible but he seemed disinclined to use the Caller-ID function on his phone and spelled names the way they sounded to him. This was fine for names like Nancy Smith, but names like Renee Ouellette became Renay Willett.

And then there were the random phone numbers and emails and addresses.

So, she was a little satisfied when she figured out which one was Hans Vernon. Her internet search for Vernon had yielded no results which had led to the twenty minute search for relevance on James's note.

She started up her truck, buckling up. She was at Vernon's place inside of ten minutes. When she neared, she realized her phone sleuthing had been pointless. There was a small army present. Men and women were shouting and holding signs. There were three police cars, not including James's unmarked sedan which was sitting in the driveway. The patrolmen were trying to herd people away, with very little luck.

Kaori turned off her truck, unbuckled and got out. She stood for a few moments, one foot still in the vehicle, staring over the top.

Mobs were truly ugly. She remembered the recent riots in Baltimore. But that had seemed so far away. Not something that could happen in a sweet little town like hers. But she knew that all towns had secrets. Secrets got into the darkest places and grew, unchecked, like nightmares or fungus. She thought about her own life and wondered what secrets people could find there.

She closed the door to her truck and pulled out her phone, keying up the recorder. Most people knew she was a reporter and when she slipped into the edges of the mob, it was only too easy to get them to talk to her. She took names, contact information and statements from over a dozen people. She saved each recording separately, labeling it. She knew she would probably go over her phone quota this month but it would be worth it.

She was getting ready to take a statement from a teenaged boy, when a hand fell on her shoulder and spun her around. She found herself facing Sean Wisneski, her ex. He did not look happy.

"Hey, Sean," she said cheerfully, disengaging herself from his grip. She started past him, back toward her truck.

"What are you doing here?" he asked.

What do you mean?" she asked over her shoulder.

"I called you. I told you not to pursue this. Evans is covering the disappearance."

She had gotten the message he'd left on her cell. It was part of what had galvanized her into her current course of action. "Weird. I never got the message. Oh well. I have statements. I'll be happy to share them with Evans if he wants to share his by-line."

"Evans would rather fester and rot than share a by-line with you," Sean said.

Kaori doubted Evans, a jovial father of three who always

invited Kaori to family picnics and delighted in talking gossip with her, had actually said that.

"Freedom of the press," she said. "You're always harping on about it. I can write anything I want."

"I'm not going to print it."

They were at her truck by now. She unlocked it. "Then, I'll sell it to another paper." She wasn't entirely sure what she was saying. She felt exhilarated, on fire. It was a heady feeling and she could see why some journalists said that the story chose you.

"You wouldn't dare," Sean said.

"Let's wager on that, then," she said, moving to unlock her truck. She felt Sean's hand descend on her shoulder, the grip tightening. Then it was gone. She turned around in surprise. Her surprise was compounded when she saw who had grabbed Sean. Eric Stevens, James's partner and the only other detective in the PIPD.

"Get lost, leech," Eric said, pushing Sean away. Sean was a tall guy, almost six feet, but he was stick thin. Eric looked like he occasionally moonlighted for the NFL. Sean looked like he was thinking about a tussle, but then shrugged and walked off. Kaori knew she hadn't heard the end of this.

"Thanks, Eric," she said.

"If he bothers you again, let me or Pritchard know." Eric adopted a thoughtful expression. "On second thought, just let me know. Pritchard is likely to do something regrettable," he rumbled in his deep bass.

"Here I thought you didn't like me," she joked.

"I tolerate you," he said, patting her head in a condescending manner. She felt like a dog, which, she was sure, was the point. "And I only do that because Pritchard is in —"

"What's going on?"

Eric broke off and looked around. Kaori did too. She saw James heading their way. When she got a good look at the expression on his face, she knew she was in for a lecture.

"Just keeping the peace," Eric said. "I'll leave the renegade reporter to you." He slipped past James and started back to the mob. Kaori watched him go. She couldn't help the feeling that he'd been close to saying something important.

James paid him no mind, his eyes for Kaori alone. "What are you doing here?"

"Reporting," she said.

"I know for a fact that you're not on this story," he said.

"Freedom of the press," she said. "I can do whatever I like. Just because Sean is going to bump me to the beauty pageant circuit after this, doesn't mean I can't give it a try."

"You're not suited for this kind of work," he said. "You told me so yourself."

"I still deserve a try," she said then realized exactly what he'd said earlier. "Wait, how do you know I'm not on this story?"

"I called Sean and asked him to pull it from you."

Her vision flickered red. She had never had much of a temper but James was the one person she thought she could count on. He was supposed to be her best friend. She shoved him as hard as she could. "You told him to take this away from me? You had no idea I was even going to pursue it. I have a right to, you know!"

"I know. And I saw that look on your face in the car yesterday. I also heard from Mrs. Douglas. She called me earlier, very bent out of shape and wondering why the hell I wasn't doing anything about that little Asian reporter. Her words were a lot less child friendly, I assure you."

So Mrs. Douglas had called the cops after all. Good to know, Kaori thought ruefully. But it didn't answer the question. "Then, what do you think you're doing? You're supposed to have my back, James. You're supposed to be my best friend."

"I am your best friend," he snapped. "Which is why I will not watch you waste your life and your talents at a crappy little newspaper in the middle of nowhere."

"And what about you?" she demanded. "What about the job in Portland?"

He flinched back. "I didn't think you knew about that."

"That you got offered a job with the Portland Police? Of course I do. I'm your best friend, you moron. And it's not a crappy little paper. It's my paper."

He recovered and his gaze was steel when he looked down at her. It was her turn to recoil from the vehemence in his gaze.

"No, it's not," he said steadily. "It's his newspaper. It's your safety net, but his paper. You just work for him. You're not still married to him."

She wanted to slap him and she almost did. Instead she turned and got into her truck. She pulled out, leaving marks on the pavement. Halfway home, she pulled out her cell and called the police department. Daphne answered on the first ring.

"Daphne? I need you to go onto James's desk and eat all his cookies," she said and hung up. It was a childish, petty thing to do, but she felt better.

25
The Father

The phone rang Saturday morning. Ralph answered it on the third ring. "Hello."

"This is Detective Pritchard."

"Detective Pritchard. You have good news, I hope."

"Sorry, no news yet. We haven't been able to find Andrew's phone, nor the guy who called you on it. Have you had any trouble getting the ransom money together?"

"No. I have it. I'm just waiting for the kidnapper to call me back. I've called my investigator in on this, too."

"Good. I need to speak to Andrew again."

"Is there some problem?" asked Ralph.

"I can't say until I have him clear up a couple things he said about the day Melony went missing."

"What do you need to know?"

"I really need to talk to Andrew. Please bring him by the station, let's say, in about a half-hour."

"Fine. You do know that I'll be there when you question him? Not only as his father, but also as his lawyer, if it comes to that."

"No problem. I understand completely. See you soon."

Ralph hung up the phone and called Andrew down from his

room. "I just got a call from the police. They want me to bring you to the station."

"What for?" asked Andrew, avoiding eye contact.

"They didn't give any specifics. They just wanted to go over your whereabouts on the day Melony went missing."

"I already told them."

"I know what you said. But it seems they aren't quite sold on your story. Is there anything you want to say before we leave? If so, you'd better speak now."

"No, not really."

Ralph had interviewed many people over his thirty odd years as a lawyer and he could usually tell when they were trying to hide something or lying. Right now he was sure Andrew was doing one or the other, or maybe even both.

Ralph and Andrew drove to the station. Pritchard met them at the entrance. After exchanging greetings, he took them to a side room, shut the door, and motioned for them to have a seat.

"What's this all about?" asked Ralph.

"After some checking, it seems your son's account and my information don't match. I need to ask him some questions. Is that all right?"

"As long as I can be here, I have no problem with it. I'm sure we can clear everything up easily," said Ralph.

"You have any problem with that, Andrew?" asked the detective.

"Ah, I... I guess not." answered Andrew, looking over to his father.

Pritchard took a small notebook from his back pants pocket, flipped through a few pages, and then scanned the information he had written.

"You said you were late picking Melony up because of a delay at your school."

"Yes, that's right," said Andrew.

"According to a couple eyewitnesses, your vehicle was seen at Melony's school just before three."

"You sure it was my car?"

"Not too many green cars with orange driver's-side front fenders roaming around this town."

"I'm telling you I didn't get there until around 3:25 or 3:30 PM," said Andrew, panic creeping into his voice.

"Andrew are you sure you got the times right?" interjected Ralph.

"Yes, Dad. I'm sure," said Andrew.

Ralph could tell that Andrew wasn't telling the truth about something by the way he fidgeted in his seat and kept looking at the floor and ceiling.

"Andrew, do you have anyone that can validate your story of being at your school until then?" asked the detective.

"Ah, I don't think so. I really don't know," said Andrew.

"You mean that you had to stay at school for whatever reason, but no one saw you?"

"Yeah. It was something I had to check on for a project," answered Andrew.

"Andrew, right now, you've become the lead suspect of your sister's disappearance. So if you have anything to take away that suspicion, you'd better tell it," said Ralph. His voice was stern and contained a hint of anger.

"Your father is right," said Detective Pritchard. "If you picked up Melony, had an argument, and ended up doing something to her, now is the time to say."

"I didn't do anything to her. Honest. Dad, I'm telling the truth. Why don't you believe me?"

"I do, but I can also see the detective's viewpoint. So, I think now is the time to come clean on what you were doing on that day. Otherwise, as much as I don't want to, I might have to agree with the detective," said Ralph.

Andrew looked at his father and then Pritchard. "I don't want to get anyone in trouble."

"Can't be any more trouble than you're getting into right now," said Ralph.

"I couldn't have been at Melony's school just before three, because I was down below the bike path with some friends."

"What were you doing there?" asked the detective.

"If I tell you, what will happen to us?" asked Andrew, fear filling his voice.

"Depends on how serious it was. I can't determine that until

I know," said Pritchard.

"Just tell us. Whatever it was, we'll deal with it. Right now, finding out what happened to your sister is more important," said Ralph, calm had come back into his voice as he switched over to lawyer mode.

"Okay. Some friends and I were there smoking some weed," said Andrew. His head fell into his hands on the table.

"Who was with you?" asked Detective Pritchard.

"Do I have to tell? They'll kill me if I do."

"Not really much choice. It's the only way that your story can be verified," said Pritchard.

Andrew looked at his father. Ralph just nodded.

"Martin Doles, Jen March, and some lady I never met before named Elma, or Elly, or some E name. I don't recall. She's the one that had the weed. She took one hit, gave it to Martin, took off for about five minutes, and then returned and stayed until we all left. That's the truth," said Andrew.

Detective Pritchard sat quietly for a moment. Then he looked Andrew in the eye and asked, "Can I see your cell phone?"

A look of panic came over Andrews face, as he looked up at his father. "I lost it."

"When did you lose it?" Pritchard asked.

"Must have been Thursday," said Andrew.

"Where was it that you last saw it?"

"I left it in my car when I got to school. I got banned from taking it inside for violating the 'no texting in class' rule."

Detective Pritchard gave Andrew a I'm-not-buying-it look. "You sure you didn't give or loan it to someone?"

"No way. Someone must have taken it," answered Andrew, frustration showing on his face.

"You keep your car locked?" asked Pritchard.

"Yes."

"Then how could it go missing or get stolen?" asked an equally frustrated looking Pritchard.

"When I returned to the car, after meeting with my friends, I noticed my keys weren't in my pocket. I retraced my steps along the path but couldn't find them. When I returned to the car

I found them laying on the ground by the rear tire. I guess I dropped them when I threw my books in the back seat before I went down the path. Maybe, someone used them to get the phone," said Andrew, hoping this would clear up the situation.

"So let's see; you didn't show up at school until almost 3:30 PM, but your car was seen there at around three. Your phone has gone missing from the locked car, but you don't know how. I'm not really buying any of this right now. Unless you got some better explanation, you just jumped to the top of my suspect list," said Pritchard.

"Detective, aren't you being a little quick here?" asked Ralph.

"Just following the evidence, Counselor."

"Unless you're going to charge him with something, I think we're done here for the day," said Ralph, getting up and motioning Andrew to do the same.

"Can't make any charges stick right now, so he's free to go. But I may call him back any time. Do you understand?"

"Yes, I do. I'll be sure to have Andrew available if needed. I'm sure he has told the truth," said Ralph.

Ralph and Andrew didn't speak on the way home. Andrew just stared out the window. Ralph looked straight ahead, driving. Once in the house, Ralph told Andrew to go to his room and they would talk more later. Andrew shrugged and went upstairs.

'What is wrong with that boy and is he telling the truth?' thought Ralph, as he picked up his phone to call Frank.

26
The Private Investigator

Frank Bishop hung up his phone, jotted some information on a piece of paper, and placed it in the Harper folder. 'This case is getting stranger all the time. Missing kid, burned body, and now, a strange call from Andrew's phone asking for ransom. Hopefully Ralph will have more information,' Frank thought.

Frank tossed his cigarette on the pavement, crushed it beneath his shoe and headed up the walkway to the Harper's house. By the time he got to the door Ralph had already opened it.

"Glad you could make it," said Ralph

"No problem. I'll tell you what I've found out so far," said Frank.

"Okay."

Frank pulled a notepad from his jacket pocket, flipped through a few pages, and studied the notes he had jotted down. "Hmmm! Let's see. I talked to your neighbor, Randall Snow, and he said he seen someone leaving your house around three AM, Thursday. Even though he didn't see the person's face, he assumed it was Andrew. He said it was strange that Andrew didn't take the car but walked to the end of the street and disappeared. When I questioned him about Melony's disappearance he said he suspects that Andrew had something to do with it. I questioned him why he thought that and he replied that Andrew had to be the last to see her since he picked her up from school the day she went missing. I mentioned that Andrew said he was late and Melony was gone when he got to the school. Snow was sure he seen Andrew's car at the school at around three PM while he was waiting for his kids. I asked if he was sure it was Andrew's car and he said it definitely was. No one could mistake that car, especially with that orange front fender. He had just assumed Andrew was driving. With that information I went to the school, but didn't get much. A couple kids who heard me asking about Melony came up to me and told me the last time they saw her, she was getting into Andrew's car. I asked at what time and they said the usual time around three PM. So according to what I can tell either Andrew is lying or someone else had his car. That's about all I have for now. You told me about the call, but I need as many details as you can give me. Start from the beginning," said Frank, closing the notepad.

Ralph spoke, "I was on my way home from Augusta when I received a call from Andrew's cell phone. It was a disguised voice, a man's, claiming to have Melony or at least know about her. He said that the burned body could have been her and who knows what could happen in the future. He demanded $250 thousand, laughed, and hung up."

"Well, it's easy to disguise voices these days. Did he say anything that may help in identifying him?"

"He called me JAG, so it's probably someone that knows I was a lawyer in the Navy. Of course, Andrew would know that, too."

"You have any idea who from your JAG days would have a grudge against you?"

"I anticipated that question, so I went through some of the cases I prosecuted back then. There were only four. I did mostly defense work and consulting on wills and such. Because I prosecuted so few cases, I'd already collected the information in case I decided to apply for work at the State Attorney's office."

Ralph opened his laptop, booted it up, and pulled up a file ,'cases prosecuted as a JAG' and clicked through documents. "First case: Hugo Spanner, 2nd Class Supply Clerk, four years for misappropriation of government property. Second case: Lt. Larry Gilmore, Dispersing Officer, six years for fraud and theft. He actually created a person, had their pay go to direct deposit and withdrew it under the false name. Third case: Jeffrey Baxter, 2nd Class Gunner's Mate, four years for drug trafficking on base. When he got out the Virginia State DA charged him for selling off base. Fourth case, Hiram Driscoll, 1st Class Machinist Mate, ten years for beating his girlfriend's lover to death. Of the four, he's the only one that threatened me."

"Let me take these names and see if I can find out where they are today. It may give us a lead. Hate to ask, but what about Andrew? Can he explain how his phone was used?"

"First he said he left it in his car, but when we were interviewed by Detective Pritchard, Andrew confessed that his phone must have been lost or stolen. Andrew claimed it happened on Thursday, the day Melony went missing."

"Do you believe him?"

"I know it looks bad, but yes I do. He may be a mixed up teenager, but I don't think he could harm his sister."

"I hope you're right. I'll get to checking these suspects right away. I'll let you know what I find out. By the way, do you have Andrew's phone number? I'll need to do some checking on that, too."

"Anything else?" asked Frank.

"One other thing that may help you, Andrew told the Detective that he and some friends were smoking weed and that's why he was late getting to Melony's school. Also, I've scraped together the money for the ransom. I'm just waiting for the kidnappers to call again."

"You got these so-called friends' names?"

Ralph gave Frank the phone numbers and the names of the two people that were with Andrew Thursday afternoon.

At the door, Ralph said, "Thanks for coming. And one more thing: could you keep a closer eye on Andrew, just in case?

"Sure. Talk to you later."

Frank drove home, went straight to his basement office, and turned on his computer. While he waited for it to boot, he picked up his desk phone, pushed a speed dial button, and hoped for a familiar voice to answer. On the third ring he got his wish.

"Morning, Sweetheart. How's it going today," he asked, with a slight chuckle.

"Don't sweetheart me, you jerk," was the reply.

"Now, Clara. You know I love ya, Gal," he said, a full laugh this time.

"You love no one but Frank Bishop. You know it and so does everyone else. What does your sweet talking butt want now?" Clara asked, letting out a chuckle of her own.

"I need some information on a call from a cell phone. Where it came from or at least the area of the tower it pinged off from."

"You know I'm not suppose to do that without a court order. We go through this every time. Besides, it's Saturday and I'm at home."

"I know Sweetie, but this involves that girl that went missing on Thursday. You do know she has diabetes, so I don't really have time for formalities. Being at home has never hindered you before, as I recall."

"You always have some angle to play. Give me the number and I'll see what I can do. If I get in trouble, I'm taking you down with me. So be forewarned."

"Wouldn't have it any other way, Dear. And thanks. I owe you one."

"One? This makes about twenty if I count right. And believe me, one day I'm going to collect."

"I'm sure you will. Let me know what you find out. I hate to rush you but I need it ASAP, or sooner."

"I know. When do you ever not?"

Frank hung up the phone. 'Clara, now there was a true sweetheart. Probably one of the best at tracing calls in the state. She's been my go-to for forever, I think,' Frank said to himself, as he turned his attention to his computer. Spanner was living in

California and, according to his social media pages, was at a Laker's game. Gilmore had died in a crash two years ago. Baxter was doing time in upstate New York on drug charges. He had one more name from Ralph's list to search: Driscoll. He typed in the name and waited for the computer to respond. Six names came up. Four were over 70 so that left two. The first one he checked was a farmer in Iowa. The second one had about six different addresses in the last five years. Frank went to the background history page and typed in the name. Within minutes, he had plodded through all the garbage and, 'bingo', he had what he wanted. Driscoll served a combined ten years in Federal and military prison for murder. 'This has to be our guy. But where is he now?' Under relatives was listed his parents, both deceased, a sister, who happened to live in Mars Hill, Maine, and a son, whereabouts unknown. Frank shut down his computer, and drove to the sister's address.

He walked up the steps of the ragged looking house, knocked on the door and waited. An old lady from the next house over approached him.

"If you're one of her clients, she ain't home," said the woman, eyeing Frank suspiciously.

"Not a client. Just got a couple questions for her. Would you happen to know when she'll be back?"

"Nope, she left yesterday. Said something about going to a Red Sox game, laughed, and took off."

"Anything strange happen here recently?"

"This whole place is strange. But nothing unusual that I can tell. Men come and men go. That's all I know."

"Anyone seem to stay longer than normal?"

"Some guy came by early Thursday morning and they left together later in the day. He in his car, she in hers. She seen me looking and spouted something about him being her brother or some crazy thing like that."

"You happen to know her last name?"

"Pierce, Emily Pierce. She got divorced a few years back but kept her married name. Poor guy. He was a nice person. Didn't deserve to be hooked up with the likes of her."

Frank wrote the info in his book, got back in his car, and

headed home. Once there, he checked his messages. There were two, both from Clara. He picked up the phone and dialed back.

"What you got for me, Sweetheart?" he asked, when she picked up the phone.

"Took a bit, but I got the info you wanted."

"Ok! Let me have it."

"The call came from mid-coast. It pinged first off a tower in the Calais area then off three others before it reached Ralph's cell."

"Thank you very much, Sweetheart. You may have just helped save a little girl's life."

"I doubt it, but I do hope you find her safe,"

Frank next called the home of his friend, Irene, who worked at the DMV. Though the office was closed Saturdays, she, like Clara, had 'other' means of finding the information he needed. He'd never asked either woman what those means entailed and they'd never offered. He asked her to get him the license plate numbers for both Emily and Driscoll. "Can you get them for me, Lovely Lady?"

"You can stop with the sweet talk. I'm accessing their records right now. Getting Emily's number is easy, but Driscoll seems to change his license like a teenage girl changes clothes: often. The last listing is from Massachusetts. The Back Bay Area of Boston. Anything else you need?"

Frank wrote down the two numbers and said "No, I think this will do it for now. Thank you, my sweet Irene. Take care." He hung up the phone and dug through an old address book for Ed Wills, his partner before his ex-wife insisted they move up north. 'I'll owe so many favors, I'll never get back to even, let alone have some in the bank for later use,' thought Frank as he dialed Ed's phone number.

"Ed Wills, P.I. for all your needs. How may I help you?"

"Ed, you old sea dog. How's it going?"

"Okay. And who might you be?"

"It's your worst nightmare, Frank Bishop."

"Frankie boy! Long time. How you doing?"

"Not bad."

"I know you didn't call just to say 'Hi', so what do you

want?"

"Got a favor, more like a job, for you."

"As long as you're paying, I'm all ears. You know my motto: 'No pay, no play.'" Ed chuckled.

"How could I forget? It's the same one all the street girls in Boston use. I think you taught it to them."

"Okay, okay. What's the job?"

"Need you to track down the where-abouts of a guy named Hiram Driscoll for me. His last known address is in the Back Bay Area of your great city."

"What did he do?"

"My client's daughter has gone missing and I like this jerk as the prime pervert to have taken her. Seems he has a grudge against my client."

"Grudge revenge, that's one of the worst things as far as I'm concerned. Fax or e-mail me the complete info and I'll get right on it," said Ed, giving Frank his fax number and e-mail address.

"It's on the way. And need I tell you that this a 'we needed it yesterday' thing. The girl is a diabetic and time is running out. I'm also sending you the guy's license plate number along with his sister's, who may or may not be involved. Maybe you can give them to some of your contacts at the police stations and have them be on the lookout."

"Got it."

Frank hung up the phone and turned his attention to his notes on Andrew. He didn't think Andrew harmed Melony but he promised to keep an eye on the boy. He might as well get started verifying Andrew's alibi.

Frank snubbed out his smoke and immediately lit another. 'These are going to kill me one day,' he thought, as he studied the notes in front of him.

27
The Reporter

Kaori woke up Saturday afternoon from her nap with a stiff neck and a pounding head. At least she thought it was her head, then she realized it was someone at the door. She looked blearily at her laptop. She had fallen asleep in the middle of writing the foundation of the article. She rubbed her cheek and felt the imprint from the keys embossed there. On the computer screen there was a string of unintelligent characters. She deleted them and got to her feet, rubbing her neck.

The pounding at the door was getting more insistent and she made her way up the stairs that led to the side door. She opened it and glared at James.

"Go away," she croaked.

"You haven't seen the news, have you?" he asked. He shoved past her, not unkindly. He looked haggard and she looked at her watch.

"What the —"

"Have you heard the news?" he asked again.

"No," she admitted as he made his way down the stairs into her living room. He snatched up the remote and turned on the TV, navigating through the channels. Finally he left off on a news station. Kaori stood, watching the broadcast. At some point she sat down.

"Are you serious?" she gasped.

James said, "Hans Vernon's house was burned to the ground. He's in intensive care at The Aroostook Medical Center," he said. His voice was flat.

"Arson?" she asked.

"Not confirmed, but probably."

"Did you know this would happen?" she asked quietly.

"I didn't. But they teach you about mob mentality in the academy," he said. "You don't go into a situation like this without considering all the possibilities."

She rubbed her arms, feeling cold for some reason.

He got onto the couch with her, nabbing the quilt from the back of the couch. He took her in his arms, her back to his chest. He wrapped the quilt around them and she relaxed. She always felt safe in his arms. She had never felt this way with her ex-husband. It had been like being with a childhood friend she wasn't in love with anymore. It was like burning hot and fast, like a grease fire that left you feeling empty after.

But it had always felt like a haven with James. She closed her eyes.

When she woke again, she was still in James's arms and it was Sunday morning. When she disengaged herself, she saw the lines of exhaustion on his face, even asleep. She reached out and smoothed his hair down.

She changed as quickly and quietly as she could. She pulled a gingersnap from the stack of cookies she'd squirreled away the night before and set it on James's chest. She knew he would resent her for what she was about to do. She herself knew it bordered on disrespectful. But she had to know. Did Vernon take Melony? Had he killed her to cover it up? If so, then he deserved prison. Maybe Melony had lapsed into a coma when she didn't get her medicine. Vernon could have panicked. What if he hadn't meant to hurt her? Was he innocent? There were any number of variables. She had to speak with him.

She rubbed her arms. It was cold outside but she didn't go back for a jacket. She recognized that she had to do this now or not at all.

A hand fell on her shoulder.

She looked around. James looked annoyed. He had the cookie in his shirt pocket.

"I was just —" she began.

"I know," he said. "But they aren't going to let a reporter speak to Vernon. I need to talk to him, anyway. Get in. I'll drive."

Kaori watched the interview through the observation window. Vernon looked her way several times, chewing on his lower lip. She found her mind wandering. It wasn't that she wasn't interested in the story. She knew that pedophiles could go to extreme measures to get their hands on the right kid, but this seemed wrong somehow. It was sounding like Hans Vernon knew nothing about Melony. She ran her mind over what James had told her of Andrew's interview. The hot older woman, the weed. Losing his phone. Going to pick up Melony. Finding her missing. It was sounding more like someone had planned this. Someone had gone to lengths to get their hands on the girl.

It had to come back to the dad. It just had to.

The interview was now over. James met Kaori in the hospital hallway. "So?"

"Harper was military," she said.

"Yeah. We knew that. What's that got to do with Hans Vernon?"

"Not a thing. Harper was pretty high up in the military."

James had the expression of someone trying not to roll their eyes. "Yes. That is a fact."

"So, don't military men make enemies too?" she asked.

28
The Private Investigator

Late Sunday morning, Frank Bishop waited across from the Birch Street apartment complex. He checked his watch and crushed out another smoke. 'Got to give these thing up before they kill me.' He hacked up phlegm and spit it out. Around 12:15 PM his quarry appeared. He followed the boy to the tree area below the bike path.

"Martin Doles," Frank yelled.

A thin, sandy haired boy turned around, noticed Frank, and took off running. Frank closed the gap and grabbed the boy. He spun the kid around and moved his hand from Doles's back collar to his neck and pushed him against a tree.

"What you running from?" asked Frank, tightening his grip.

"Are you a cop? I told you guys everything I know earlier this morning," the boy said, barely audible due to pressure on his throat.

"No, I'm not a cop. Why would such an upstanding boy as yourself be afraid of the police?" Frank asked, a sadistic grin crossing his lips.

"No reason. I just don't like them."

Frank loosened his grip, looked the boy in the eye, and in a threatening tone said, "I'm going to ask you a few questions and the answers will be the determining factor of how much or how little pressure I apply. Do you understand?"

Martin nodded. Frank reached into his pocket and took out a picture.

"You know this woman?" asked Frank. He showed Martin an old mugshot of Emily.

"No."

Franks hand tightened more. "You sure?"

Martin motioned for Frank to loosen his hold. "Okay, okay. I've seen her around now and then. Her name is Emy, or Ellen, or something like that. I don't really know her that well. I've seen her at Kyle's place a few times." He gasped for air.

"Kyle who?"

"I don't know his last name or even if that's his real name. He's just a guy I buy weed from. That woman has been there a couple times."

"When was the last time you saw her?"

"Thursday after school. She was waiting in the parking lot when I got there. She asked if I was interested in some free weed. I would never turn down free weed."

"What else did she want? No one gives that stuff away these days."

"She asked if I knew Andrew Harper and wanted me to get him to come with us. So when Andrew came out of the school, I told him about the weed. He was hesitant at first, but Jen talked him into coming along. He dropped his books in his car and we all headed down to the area below the bike path."

"Anything else happen?" Frank asked, releasing Martin's throat.

"Not that I can think of. At one point, she left for about five minutes. Something about getting something from her car."

"How long were you guys there?"

"Maybe a half hour, but it could have been less. We heard a car horn and the woman got a strange look on her face. You know, one like you just did something evil. She said she had to leave and took off. That's all, I swear."

"Okay. You best be telling the truth or I'll come back and you *will* regret it," said Frank, narrowing his eyes. "One more thing. Where does this Kyle live?"

"He'd kill me if I told," said Martin, fear in his eyes.

"And I'll hurt you if you don't." Frank grabbed onto Martin's wrist and threatened with a fist.

"Green apartment house on Mechanic Street. Top floor. Number six," said Martin, breaking free and taking off at a full run.

Frank returned to his vehicle and drove to the apartment building. It didn't take long for him to find it. He parked right in front, checked his gun, and climbed the stairs to Apartment six. He knocked on the door, waited a bit, and then banged on it for at least ten seconds.

"Hold on, hold on. I'm coming," said a gravelly voice from inside.

A short, skinny man with unkempt hair and beard and wearing nothing but a dirty pair of shorts answered the door. He squinted at Frank and mumbled "Yeah?"

Frank could tell the man was wasted on something. He growled. "You Kyle?"

The guy stepped back and started to shut the door, but Frank blocked the attempt with his foot. He reached in and grabbed the guy by the hair.

"Last time I'll ask politely. Are you Kyle?" asked Frank, pulling the guy halfway out the door.

"You a cop?"

"No. Just looking for someone. Ever see this woman before?" asked Frank, pulling the picture from his pocket. Moving his jacket back exposing his gun, he said, "Don't try lying to me. 'Cause if you do, you'll regret it."

"I've seen her a few times. We do business on occasion."

"When was the last time you saw her?"

"Thursday. She came by and said she needed some weed for a special occasion."

"She say what that was?"

"No, didn't say and I didn't ask. When she left, I said I'd see her next week and she said probably not. I asked why and she told me she was heading south. I inquired for what and she told me for a vacation, maybe even go see the Sox play. Then she laughed and took off. That's everything."

"Best be speaking the truth or I'll come back and turn you into a screaming girl," said Frank, pushing Kyle back into the apartment.

Frank returned to his car, dialed a number on his cell phone, and waited.

"Presque Isle Police Department, how may I help you?"

"Yes, this is Frank Bishop could you connect me with Detective Sergeant Harrison from the drug investigation unit, please." As Frank waited he thought, 'Poor Kyle what a surprise he has coming. I almost feel sorry for him. Nah, I really don't.'

Frank told Harrison about Kyle. When he hung up, he called Ralph to meet him for the afternoon flight from Presque Isle to Boston.

During the flight Frank brought Ralph up to speed on his investigation. His contact in Calais had found Andrew's phone. The person, presumably Driscoll, had thrown the phone in a trash can and a teen had found it. It had been sent to Augusta but Frank didn't think they would get any useful info off it. Thus, he decided to make the trip to Dricoll's last know habitat to see if it would lead anywhere.

Inside the Boston terminal they both checked their phones. Neither had any pressing calls, so they proceeded to the rental car lot and headed to their hotel. Once settled in, Ralph called Detective Pritchard to ensure he got the word on Andrew's phone, hoping it would at least clear that part up. Frank called Ed.

"Ed, my friend. What's going on."

"Not much. What can I do for you?"

"You still got the address for Driscoll?"

"Yep, somewhere in all the papers on my desk."

"Could you dig it up? I need it."

"What you gonna do with it way up there, in no-man's land?"

"I'm in Boston, actually. I want to go see if I can get a lead on this guy."

"In Boston? Great. We should get together for a drink. Go over old times."

"Sounds good, but can't do it right now. If I'm still in Boston once this case is over, I'll be sure to look you up and we'll do the drink thing."

"I fully understand. Hope we can do it, though. Would be nice. Give me a second and I'll get the address for you."

Frank stared at the address on the slip of paper he had taken from his pocket.

"Looks like this is the place," he said to Ralph.

"The place sure looks like a dump," said Ralph.

"What do you expect from a presumed lowlife like this guy?"

The apartment house had seen better days. It needed a paint job, the stoop revamped, or a complete demolition. It was one of the average buildings on the block. A few wine bottles and empty cigarette packs lay strewn around the steps and along the building's front.

An older man holding a brown paper bag sat on the stoop staring at the two. "You fellows looking for something?"

"We're looking for a guy that goes by the name of Hiram Driscoll? Would he happen to live here?" asked Frank.

"That, he does."

Seeing that the man was not forthcoming with an abundance of information, Frank continued on. "Would he happen to be home?"

"Nope."

"Would you know when he might be back?"

"Nope."

Frank realized that it would take forever getting information at this rate. He reached in his pocket and pulled out a twenty. Waved it in front of the man and said, "This is all yours, if you could be a little more explicit."

The man eyed the bill and reached for it. Frank pulled the twenty back, just out of the man's reach.

"You talk first. Then, you get the money," Frank said, a sadistic smile on his face.

"He lives here, but has been gone since last Monday afternoon. Never told anyone where he was off to, mostly because no one even asked or cared."

"Do you know if he had a job or any place he might have hung out?"

"Don't know where he spent his time, but he did have a job working for some construction company. If the name on his shirt was true, it was Henderson's from over Charlestown way."

Frank handed the guy the twenty, motioned to Ralph, and headed to the car.

"I think you just wasted a twenty on that guy," said Ralph.

"Ralph, you best get your head on straight. Stop clouding your mind with brooding about Melony and start thinking of why we're here. Even though we didn't find Hiram, we did get a starting point. We'll locate Henderson's Construction and go from there."

"You're right. I have been preoccupied with thinking of everything but what's going on right now. So, let's go find Henderson's Construction," said Ralph shaking his head, as if to clear the cobwebs clouding his thought process.

"Being that it's a Sunday evening, we'll have to wait until tomorrow to see someone. Meanwhile, let's grab something to eat and set our game plan."

"Sounds good," said Ralph. "If I don't become a nervous wreck first."

29
The Kidnapper

Late Sunday night, Hiram Driscoll stood in the dusty main room of the warehouse. He pursed his lips. The most recent fight with his sister, Emily, left him filled with dread. All along, he'd told her his plan. He was taking Harper's kid to replace his own. It was only right, since Harper had, in effect, taken his son.

Emily wasn't listening, though. She had her own agenda and it was now apparent that she'd had it from the start. She'd lost everything, too, when Harper had locked him up. She'd been fired from a good job as a clerk at a prestigious law firm and could find no employment except as a bar girl at a local club. She'd lost her newly purchased house, too, when she couldn't make the payments. She still had her car, but he wasn't sure how she'd managed to scrape together enough money for the payments.

She'd never said anything to him about it. Clearly, she held Harper responsible for the drastic turn her life had taken. And Harper *was* responsible. But, she wanted more than revenge, more than reimbursement. She wanted to burn him, and everything he had or loved, all the way into the ground.

She was an Emily he didn't know.

Driscoll pulled the key out of his pocket, turning it over and over in his hand. Then, mind made up, he strode to Melony's door and unlocked it. The girl sat slumped against the chair in the center of the room, looking up at him with fevered eyes. He walked in, pulled her to her feet, and took her by the wrist. She said nothing, following him meekly, as if she knew he was her only lifeline. He tossed her backpack at her as they passed the table.

Together they crossed the abandoned warehouse, stepping around bits of trash and rat droppings. When they reached the old wooden exit door, he stopped and listened. Nothing from the other side. Sliding the door open, he came face-to-face with Emily silhouetted against the dark night.

"Where are you taking her?" Emily's voice was hard, like steel.

"I don't want her to die. I'm going to keep her." He pushed Melony behind him with one hand, holding her hand with the other.

"Hiram, we talked about this several times. We agreed — "

"No. We didn't. You made the decision and bullied me into it. Well, I don't agree. I'm keeping her. She's going to replace what Harper took from me. She's going to replace my boy." He circled Emily, pushing and pulling Melony to stay behind him. "With the money you get from him, you'll be able to replace your house."

"He can't erase the embarrassment and shame. Nor can he replace all those years I spent working in dive or another, doing anything just to get by. I want to make him pay for that. Don't you?" She cocked her head, narrowing her eyes, advancing.

Driscoll nodded hard, still circling to keep between his sister and Melony. "Of course, I do. You know that. Just not with *this* girl. I don't care about anything else. I'll help you do whatever you want to Harper and the rest of his family. But, this girl is mine."

With a snarl, Emily lunged around Driscoll, trying to reach Melony. He let go of the girl's tiny wrist, using both hands to stop the stranger his sister had become.

30
The Little Girl

 Melony didn't look back, but took off running, or what she thought was running. Her body felt sick and weak; it surprised her what little strength she had left. Maybe it wasn't strength, but fear, or maybe it was the small hope that she would see her family again. At the moment, she couldn't decide. All she knew, her chance to escape was now. In a way she was thankful for Emily's interruption. Otherwise, there would have been no chance to slip away.
 With only the moon's light to guide her, Melony felt along the outside walls of the abandoned warehouse. Having been confined in that small storage room, she didn't realize how big the area actually was.
 Becoming dizzier with every step, Melony stumbled around numerous crates and dumpsters. Falling a few times, she quickly picked herself up and urged herself forward.
 From a distance somewhere behind her a shot rang out. Melony jumped. Its sound echoed through her mind and lingered, reminding her of her current danger. Unsure of the distance she had made between herself and the other two, she knew that Driscoll or Emily wouldn't be too far behind. She needed to get far away from the area, and quickly.

A voice called out to her through the darkness. "Melony!"

It was Emily. She called again. And again.

Melony's heart started to race. With a good distance still between them, she urged herself onto a deserted side road. She took the next turn. Then another. This one led toward the lights of a city. It didn't look far, a few miles at most. There, she could possibly find help. Stumbling forward, Melony hurried for the city as fast as her body would allow her, the sound of Emily's voice calling her name growing fainter.

Almost an hour later, Melony found herself still wandering toward the city. Around her, the streets were filled with run down houses and rusty broken down cars. Trash spewed across several lawns and scattered in the night's chill wind. Several lampposts flickered light onto the sidewalks and cast shadows from lanky cats that scurried away, trying to find shelter from the vicious growls and barks of nearby dogs.

With sore feet, Melony ventured down one of the streets. It felt late. Way past her bed time. Not too many people were outside. The few that were didn't seem to take notice of her. Passing by one of the houses, harsh shouts could be heard coming from what sounded to be a man and woman arguing. She shivered at their temper and knew no help would come from them. From another house, a strange smell wafted heavily in the air. She did not recognize it, but it reminded her of something sweet, bitter, and smoky all mixed into one. Followed behind it came several laughs.

Now, halfway down the street, she stood before two unlit houses. One appeared vacant with several cardboard boxes piled on its white porch while some lay near its side between the two buildings. Looking to make sure that no one was around, Melony crossed over to the boxes near the side of the house and found a few that were close to her size. Thinking this the best place to hide, she crawled under one and drew herself into a tight ball, silently crying.

31
The Private Investigator

The next morning was Monday. Melony had been missing for over four days. Frank and Ralph quietly checked and answered their phone messages while waiting for their breakfast. Once they had eaten, they headed to their rental car.

"I brought the ransom money with me, but I think we can assume the kidnapper isn't going to call back. It could mean …" Ralph shook his head, took a deep breath, and started again. "Where do we start looking?"

Frank knew exactly what Ralph had been thinking: Melony could be dead. He decided it would be best not to let Ralph dwell on that thought. "I looked up Henderson's Construction in Charlestown last night, so I suppose that's where."

Neither said much on the drive to Henderson's. Frank pulled into the lot and noticed an office looking building to the right of an area that contained a number of construction vehicles. He pulled up in front, got out and went to the door that had **'OFFICE'** stenciled on the window. Ralph followed Frank inside.

"May I help you?" ask a young girl behind a desk.

"Is the owner around?" asked Frank.

"Yes, my dad is in the back. May I asked who you are?"

"I'm Frank Bishop and this is Ralph Harper. We're from Northern Maine."

"What is it that you would like to speak to Carl about?" she asked, as she wrote some information on a post-it note.

"We'd like to talk to him about a person who may have, or is currently, working here," replied Frank.

The girl excused herself and went to the back room. A couple minutes later, she returned with a short, portly man sporting a beard. He had a weathered face.

"I'm Carl Henderson, owner of this company," he said, extending his hand.

Frank and Ralph both shook his hand and exchanged greetings.

"What can I help you with? My daughter says you're looking for someone that may be employed here."

"Yes, a man named Hiram Driscoll. Have ever heard of him?" asked Frank.

"I have so many that come and go. It's hard to remember everyone."

"Here you go, Dad. We had a man by that name working for us until last Monday afternoon. According to his foreman, he left the site at noon saying he was sick. He hasn't returned, yet," said the girl, reading from her computer screen.

"Guess we did. It's funny that he hasn't returned at least to get his pay check," said Carl.

"Can you tell us where he was working last?" asked Frank.

"Let's see. Over on Ericsson Street, on a warehouse renovation," said he girl.

"Could we get the address?" asked Ralph.

The girl wrote down the site address, added the name of the job foreman, and handed the slip of paper to Carl. Carl checked it, nodded, and passed it to Frank.

"If you don't mind my asking, are you guys cops? What do you want with him?" asked Carl, with a look on his face like maybe he should have asked the questions earlier.

"We're not cops. I'm a P.I. and Ralph is a lawyer. We think this guy may have something to do with Ralph's missing daughter," said Frank.

"Ah! Well, sorry I couldn't be more help. I hope you find him and the girl."

Frank and Ralph thanked the two and returned to the car.

"To Ericsson Street," said Ralph, more of a demand than a request.

"On our way," said Frank, starting the car.

They were silent during the short trip, pulling the rental car into an empty spot on Ericsson Street within minutes. Trucks from Herderson's Construction were parked beside an old warehouse. Workers were in the process of offloading materials. Frank and Ralph exited the car and headed toward the building.

"Could you tell me where to find the foreman?" Frank asked a young man, who was hauling a cart containing a stack of drywall.

"That would be Pete. He's over in that first trailer," said the guy, pointing to a white trailer off to the side.

"Thank you," said Frank. He walked to the trailer, Ralph beside him, and knocked on the trailer door.

An older, weather-beaten man with gray hair answered. "What can I do for you fellows. I'm not hiring, if that's what you're looking for."

"You Pete?" asked Frank.

"Yep."

"I'm Frank Bishop. This is Ralph Harper. We'd like to ask you a couple of questions about an employee."

"You cops?"

"Nope. I'm a P.I. and Ralph, here, is a lawyer. We're from Northern Maine," said Frank.

"Okay. Who is it you're looking for?"

"A man named Hiram Driscoll."

"That guy. Haven't seen him since last Monday, when he left sick."

"Any idea where he might have gone?" asked Ralph.

"Nope. He just took off. I haven't seen hide nor hair of him since. Too bad, too. He was a bit strange, but a good worker."

"Strange in what way?" asked Frank.

"He never hung out with the guys, except if he was doing a job with them. Always ate by himself and spent much of his lunch hour looking at all the old buildings around here. He was very curious about them, asking if they were occupied, who owned them. Strange stuff like that."

"Any particular building that he showed special interest in?" asked Frank.

"Nope, just the area in general. If I may ask, why are you looking for him for anyway?"

Frank looked at Ralph trying to decide if they should tell Pete or not. After a moment of silence, Ralph spoke up, "We think he may have kidnapped my daughter and brought her here to Boston."

"Yeah, we're turning over the rocks to see if we can get a clue as to his whereabouts," said Frank.

"I could give you his home address if that would help. But other than that, I don't have anything else," said Pete.

"Thanks, but we've already been to his place. No luck there," said Frank.

"Then, I can't be of any help. Sorry," said Pete.

"That's okay. What little you gave us is another piece of the puzzle. Thanks, anyway," said Frank.

Frank and Ralph walked back to the car.

"Looks like another dead end," said Ralph.

"Think again, Ralph. Use your head for something besides a hat rack. The one thing I got, was that Driscoll was interested in abandoned buildings around here. This being a fairly deserted area, it may be that he was looking for a hiding place. Let's search around here."

"You're right. I'm still not thinking straight. So, where around here do we start?"

"Pick a place. One is as good as the other."

The two men stood surveying the area for a couple minutes, and then Ralph said, "Want to split up? We'll cover more ground that way."

"May be a good idea, but, if he's armed, it could be dangerous." Frank tapped Ralph on the shoulder.

"What?"

"Look over by that green building. You see that guy?"

"Yes."

"My guess, and I say only a guess, is that he's a homeless person. Hopefully he's lived in this area for a while. We'll go talk to him."

Frank and Ralph approached the man, who, upon seeing them heading his way, got up from his perch and grabbed a bat leaning against the building. He raised the bat, ready to swing. "You come any closer and I'll give you the old what for."

"Hey, be careful. You could hurt someone with that thing. We just want ask you a couple questions," said Frank, raising his hands in surrender.

Ralph followed suit.

The man lowered the bat but keep a firm grip on it. "What do you want to know?"

"You been in this area long?" asked Frank.

"'Bout three months. Ever since those construction guys came. It's good pickings wherever construction is going on."

"I'm guessing you know about everything that goes on around here, then?" asked Frank.

"Pretty much."

"Could you give us a run down of anything strange going on?" asked Frank, reaching into his pocket and extracting a twenty.

The man eyed the money. "That for me?" he asked, reaching out for it.

"Depends on how much you want to talk," said Frank.

"Whatever you want. If I know it, I'll tell you."

"Beside the workers, you notice anybody else roaming around here recently?"

"Well, one of them guys kept going into different buildings. I assumed he must have been checking out new jobs. But, I haven't seen him around during the day lately."

"Anything been happening at night, that you might have seen?" asked Ralph.

"It gets really quiet around here, once the workers leave. But, I do recall that, last Thursday, a to-do went on."

"Tell me about it," said Frank.

"Actually, it was more like Friday, maybe two or three in the morning. A car pulled up by the old Milton building. Some guy got out — mighta been the same guy — and picked up what looked to me like a sack. He took it into the building. A bit later, he came out and moved his car out of sight."

"Which one is the Milton building?" asked Frank.

"Don't get in a hurry. That's not the whole story."

"Do continue, then."

"About an hour or so later another car stopped at the same building. A lady got out, went to the door, and talked to someone. Then, she moved her car to the back, too. Friday morning the man drove off and didn't return until late that night."

"What about the woman?" asked Frank.

"I'm getting to her," said the man.

Frank was getting impatient, but he said, in a calm voice, "Okay. Continue on."

"The woman never came out Friday at all. Saturday, she took off for about an hour or so and then returned. Then, Sunday night, last night, I could hear the man and woman shouting at each other. Couldn't make out what they were saying, though. Then, I heard a loud bang, like a gunshot. The next thing I know, the woman came out and ran up and down the street, back and forth across it, looking in all the building windows. She seemed to be in a panic and kept shouting for someone. Melron, Melcum, or something like that. She searched for the better part of two hours, went back in the building, and moments later came out again. She got in her car and took off down the street that way." The man pointed the opposite way of the construction.

"Could she have been shouting Melony?" asked Ralph.

"As I said, she was scurrying around and yelling. I couldn't really make out the name, but it could have been Melony."

"Okay. Now, where is the Milton building?" asked Frank.

"It's that dirty brown one with the metal railings on the steps," said the man, this time pointing to a building about a half block away.

Frank handed the man the twenty. "You've been a big help. Thank you."

"Yes. Thank you very much," said Ralph.

Frank and Ralph headed toward the building the man had indicated. Frank was trying to figure the best way to approach without tipping off Driscoll if he was, in fact, in there. He tapped Ralph on the shoulder and nodded for him to follow, then headed toward the back of the building. As he turned the corner, he noticed a car half-hidden under a collapsed overhang. He took the small notepad he always carried and flipped through the pages, stopping and studying one midway through.

"According to the plate number Clara gave me, that is Driscoll's car," he said.

"Then, he must be around here somewhere. Hopefully he hasn't detected us yet," said Ralph.

The two checked out the car. Both tried the doors, but they were all locked. Peering through the windows, they could see a bottle and a rag on the front passenger's seat. The remains of several food wrappers had been thrown in the back.

"They're most likely holed up somewhere in this building. I think it's time we checked it out," said an anxious Ralph.

Frank went to the back entrance and tried the door. To his surprise, it was unlocked. Ralph came up behind him. Frank opened the door and, in a semi-whisper, said, "We'd best proceed as quietly as possible. I suggest you stay behind me and keep a close watch on our backs."

Ralph nodded in agreement. Frank reached under his jacket and pulled his gun from its holster, checked it, and headed into the building.

"You got a permit for that thing?" Ralph quietly asked.

"Yes, but it's no good in Massachusetts. I use the old 'better to ask for forgiveness than to beg for permission' rule." He sneered. Just inside the doorway, he stopped, getting the layout of the place. Then, he moved toward the wall to his right.

"Someone, or ones, has been in here recently. Look at the floor. You can see the prints in the dust," he whispered to Ralph, pointing at the scuff marks and bare spots that mingled among the thick dust under their feet.

There were three rooms on that level of the building. Frank pointed at the the one farthest to the left to let Ralph know that he planned to check it. Frank rechecked his gun and had Ralph open the door. Once open, Frank quickly stepped in. In a moment, he stepped back out.

"Nothing here," he whispered, nodding toward the next door down.

They repeated their actions, but this time when Frank came back out, his face was pale and he had a perplexed look.

"What's wrong?" asked Ralph.

"I think I found our guy, but I don't think he's going to be much help."

Ralph stepped past Frank and entered the room. He immediately realized what Frank's statement meant. There, sprawled across an old chair, lay a body. Blood covered the chair and the body. A red pool had formed on the floor. Someone had shot the poor, unfortunate person. Ralph stepped back into the hall. "I see what you mean. I guess we'd best call the police."

"You're right, but not right this minute. Let's have a quick look around and see if we can find anything that may help us. Once the cops start swarming around here, we'll never get anything of use from them or the scene."

Frank reached inside his jacket and pulled out a pair of surgeons gloves. He noticed the funny look Ralph shot his way. "What? I use to be a Boy Scout. You know, 'Be Prepared'. Never know when you may have to dig around, or even, let's say, enter a place uninvited." He took out a second pair and handed them to Ralph.

"Don't be moving everything helter skelter. Just sort of thumb through it. But you already know this, so let's get busy." Frank carefully lifted the wallet from the body's back pocket, checked for an ID, and then just as carefully replaced it. "Well, this is our guy. Just confirmed it by his license. So either your daughter had a gun or he had a partner and things went wrong."

32
The Father

Ralph had been checking out the room while Frank did his slight-of-hand thing with Driscoll's wallet. He didn't notice anything that seemed of much help. Just some empty food cans and drink bottles. He turned to hear what Frank was saying about the body when his eye caught an object partially hidden under the door. He picked it up and, for a moment, had to steady himself against the wall.

Frank turned. "What you got there?"

"It's … It's Melony's," stammered Ralph.

"Melony's what?" asked Frank, taking the object from Ralph.

"It's her diabetes ID bracelet."

Frank checked out the bracelet and on the back was Melony's name and address.

Ralph went into the adjoining room to look for any other evidence that Melony had been there. He called for Frank to come into the room.

"What you got now?"

"Her emergency pen. It was laying on the floor. Worst part is that it's empty, which means her health is going to start, or already has started, deteriorating soon," said Ralph. Worry and fear were thick in his voice, even though he realized she could still be alive.

"At least now we know that she was here. The questions now are where and with whom is she now. From what information I gathered from the start of this investigation, I'm putting my money on Driscoll's sister."

"Probably. But how do we find her? Boston is a big city."

"We keep looking and asking. Looking and asking. Until we find her. But it is time to put these things back as close to where we found them and call the police," said Frank, reaching for his cell phone.

When the police arrived, Ralph and Frank spent forty-five minutes with them. It took about twenty minutes of that to convince them that they had nothing to do with the death of Driscoll. The fact that Frank carried a forty-five and Driscoll was shot with a thirty-eight didn't seem to register with the Boston police. But once they jumped through that hoop, they hung around hoping to obtain any information that would help them discover what happened to Melony. Having failed at getting anything that they didn't already know they gave the police information on Melony and what they knew of Emily, including her license number.

Frank and Ralph walked toward the car.

"I'm glad to get out of there," said Ralph.

"Those guys can be anal. Lucky for us Detective Carlson arrived. Guess it's true it's good to have friends in low places," said Frank.

"If the homeless man can be even half-trusted, it's possible that no one has Melony. Yet, if that's true, where could she be?" asked Ralph.

"That, I don't have a clue. But, we're not going to find her while standing here. I suggest we comb the immediate area," said Frank.

"Together, or split up?" questioned Ralph.

"Together. We'll have to talk to anybody we encounter and I'm running out of small bills," said Frank, with a slight chuckle.

"Okay. Which way do we start?"

They were pondering their course of action when they heard, "What are you guys doing here?"

Turning, they spotted two familiar faces: Detective Pritchard and the reporter, Kaori.

"We could ask you the same question," responded Ralph.

"We're following the clues of your daughter's case. Though, it seems like we're a step behind you two," said Pritchard. "We found out about the Driscolls."

"Well, we've located Hiram Driscoll, but he'll be no help. He's dead. Shot by his sister, Emily, we assume. We were just getting ready to search this area. We believe it is possible that Emily doesn't have Melony at this moment. So, she's most likely also searching."

"Can we give you a hand?" asked Pritchard.

"Are you here legally, or as an 'interested party'?" asked Frank

"I've checked in with the local Boston PD, as required by law. Kaori is tagging along for the story. In fact, we were still at the station when the call came in about the found body. Didn't connect it with the case until someone mentioned Driscoll's name. That's when we decided to come here."

"I guess a hand would be welcome," said Ralph.

"How you want to proceed?" asked Pritchard.

"Frank and I will take North, go East, and then back here. You two go South and West, back to here. Talk to anyone you see, especially the homeless. They've been a help to us so far. Hopefully, you have money because they seldom get to the point without a ten or twenty waving in front of their eyes."

"Okay. Let's get started. We'll meet back here in about an hour so. Here's my cell number if you find anything," said Pritchard, handing Ralph his card.

Ralph and Frank both handed their cards to Pritchard.

"Good hunting," said Frank, as he and Ralph headed North.

Ralph Harper had just finished checking an alleyway and was headed back to were Frank Bishop was waiting when his cell phone rang. He pulled it from his pocket and, not recognizing the number, checked it against the card Detective

Pritchard had given him. It was the same. He quickly answered.

Pritchard said, "We found her."

"What? You found her? Where?" Ralph was so overcome with relief that he dropped his phone when he folded his hands in mock prayer and whispered 'thank you' towards the sky.

When he retrieved his phone all he heard was " — started from."

"Sorry, could you repeat that? I dropped my phone and didn't hear your last," said Ralph, turning his full attention to the call.

"We're about three blocks South and couple West of where we started," repeated Pritchard.

"What street are you on?"

"I don't see any signs around. Tell you what, I'll go back to the main drag and wait for you."

"What about Melony? Is she okay?"

"She's alive, but she seems a bit disorientated. Kaori will stay with her until you show up."

"I'm on my way," shouted Ralph.

Ralph quickened his pace to a slight jog. When he met up with Frank, he said, "They found her. They found Melony."

"That's great. Where is she?" asked Frank.

"A few blocks from where we split up. Pritchard is going to wait by the main street so we can locate them."

"Then, let's get moving," said Frank, quickening his step to be in stride with Ralph.

They got to the car and Frank drove South while Ralph keep a lookout for Pritchard. Within a couple minutes, Ralph tapped Frank on the shoulder. "There he is."

"Where?"

"On the corner, next block down."

Frank pulled the car beside where Pritchard was standing. Ralph rolled down the window and asked, "Where is she?"

"Just down that way a bit," said Pritchard, pointing down the side street.

"Get in," said Ralph.

Frank unlocked the rear door and Pritchard got in.

"Head down this street. It's a couple blocks down to the

alley." said Pritchard.

They drove about two blocks, when Pritchard said, "Here. Pull over here. She's down this alley."

Frank pulled the car to the curb and, before he could fully stop, Ralph had his door open and was getting out. The sudden stop almost sent Ralph to the curb but he managed to steady himself. He ran down the street. A short ways down he saw Kaori sitting against a building, holding something in her arms. Ralph went into a full run and closed the distance in a matter of seconds.

He grabbed his daughter from Kaori's arms and gave her a crushing hug. "Melony, Sweetie, you're safe now. Daddy is here."

Noticing that she was wavering between conscious and unconscious state, he shook her saying, "Wake up, Melony. Don't sleep, you need to stay awake."

In a weak, almost inaudible, voice Melony said, "Who are you? I don't feel very good. Can you get my dad for me? He'll know what to do."

"It's me, Melony. I'm your dad. Don't you recognize me?"

"I'm so tired. Please let me rest until Daddy gets here," she faintly whispered.

"No! You can't sleep. Please, Sweetheart, try and stay awake." Ralph pulled a sugar packet out of his shirt pocket, tore it open, and sprinkled the contents on his daughter's tongue. "She's in trouble. Probably middle stages of diabetic shock. We've got to get her to a hospital as fast as possible," said Ralph.

"Don't you have anything more to help her?" asked Kaori.

"No. Tell you the truth, I never thought that far ahead when we started this journey. Besides, even if I did, at this stage it might do more harm than good. She needs a doctor," said Ralph. The adrenalin that had fueled him since Thursday seeped away. He began to shake and weakness washed over him. He could feel himself teetering on the verge of completely losing all common sense. He also knew, at that moment, he didn't have the ability to stop himself.

Frank placed his hand on Ralph's shoulder. Ralph looked

up. The helplessness must have shown. Frank reached down and pried Melony from Ralph's arms. He turned to the others and asked, "Where's the closest hospital?"

Pritchard took out his phone, tapped some information into it, and said, "Manet Community seems to be the closest."

Taking the phone from Pritchard, Frank said, "Let's get moving. Come on, Ralph. Get it together. We're running on the clock here and time isn't standing still." He hurried to the car and put Melony in the back seat.

Ralph stood up. He mumbled to himself 'come on you idiot snap out of it.' As he followed Frank, he smacked his head with his hand to clear the fog. More alert, he got in the car and told Pritchard and Kaori to meet them at the hospital. Then, he turned to Frank and said, "What are you waiting for? Get moving."

Frank took off, following the directions on Pritchard's phone. With running two red lights, in five minutes they pulled into the hospital lot. Frank stopped at the emergency entrance and told Ralph to take Melony in. He would park the car and join him soon.

Ralph lifted Melony and, as fast as he dared, headed for the door. Inside, he went to the nurse's station and said, "I need a doctor right away. My daughter is in diabetic shock."

33
The Neighbor

Wednesday afternoon, Randal looked outside his kitchen window and saw all the decorations at the Harper house. There were pastel balloons tied to every post of the front porch with matching streamers dangling and flapping in the wind. There was a big sign over the door that read: "Welcome Home Melony" in sparkle-covered red letters.

He could only imagine what that child had gone through. Randal couldn't bear to think if the same had happened to his own daughter, Diane, who was the same age as Melony. He admired how Ralph had seemed to keep it together all the time that his little girl had been missing. Randal didn't know what he would've done. He was sure he would've lost it.

Randal had taken his kids, Christopher and Diane shopping the night before, when he found out from a neighbor that her kids were attending the welcome home party. Christopher had chosen a puzzle about puppies and Diane had chosen the latest in coloring books. They insisted on wrapping the gifts themselves.

"Dad, can we go now?" Diane asked.

"Melony hasn't arrived yet."

"All the kids are going to be inside the house waiting to surprise her." Diane's pouty face resembled that of a Care Bear.

Christopher chimed in. "Can we go, please? Can we? Please, Daddy?"

"Okay. But you must promise to behave and mind your manners," Randal said.

"I promise," the kids said in unison.

"Off you go, then. Don't forget the card that goes with the presents."

"Got it. Bye, Dad," Diane said as she left the house with her brother.

Randal watched as Diane and Christopher crossed the lawn to Ralph Harper's driveway. He saw that Diane loved the decorations, by the look on her face. Christopher tried to pry a light blue balloon loose, but his big sister tugged his shirt sleeve to keep him inline. She then grabbed him by the hand and lead him onto the porch. Diane knocked and, when a lady opened the door, the children went in the house. Randal walked into the living room and sat in his chair.

Three years ago, or even last week, he wouldn't have let his kids go over to the Harper house, because Ralph represented the insurance company in the wrongful death of his wife. They had become sworn enemies. All the dirty laundry had come out at the trial. Things that neighbors know about their neighbors, the things that keep you close, that you wouldn't want anybody else to know.

Twenty minutes went by and there was a knock at the door. Randal stood up with his cane and went to the kitchen door. It was Ralph Harper. Randal opened the door.

"Randal, I can't tell you how much it means to me to see your children in my house when Melony and I got home from the hospital." Tears of joy welled in Ralph's eyes. "Can you come over as well?"

"Well, gee…I don't know, Ralph."

"Come on, it'll be fun and Melony will be happy to see you."

"Okay, I'll go, but it doesn't mean that all is forgiven."

"Let's forget about it for today, and then take it one day at a time."

"Spoken like a true lawyer. I can agree on that."

34
The Best Friend

"Bring back the ball, Frisket!" Melony said, tossing a tennis ball to the little puppy. He bounded across the grass, kicking up dirt with his little paws in his excitement. The ball whizzed past him, bounced twice, and came to a rolling stop near a large maple tree. Frisket barked at the ball, but when it didn't respond, he growled, and took it into his mouth, bounding back to Melony.

Beth giggled as Frisket dropped the ball near their feet. "Can I throw it for him?"

Melony nodded and her friend picked it up. She threw it in a high arch which the dog ran after with a gleeful bark. Her surprise party had finished half an hour ago and Beth's mother was inside the house, chatting with her father and the neighbor, Mr. Snow.

"Melony," Beth said, "I was so scared when, you know, when you were gone." This was the first chance she'd had to talk to her.

At first, Melony didn't say anything. Instead, she looked after her dog with keen interest. Frisket picked up the ball between his razor-sharp puppy teeth.

Beth waited quietly. When Frisket returned with the ball, tail wagging every step of the way, Beth scratched behind his ears and accepted the tennis ball he deposited into her hands. But this time, instead of throwing it again, she kept petting the dog. Crouching onto the ground near him, Beth waited for her friend to say something.

"Do you remember that time that we were in the woods behind Mantle Lake Park, Beth?" Melony finally asked. "For a few minutes, we thought we were lost, because we were turned around and the sun was going down and we couldn't see? I was scared like that, but even more. Especially because you weren't there. No one was there."

Melony stopped talking and looked down at the ground. When she brought her eyes up again, she smiled at Beth. "Let's go in for some cake, okay?"

35
The Father

Ralph Harper slumped into the big easy chair after Melony's welcome home party. It had been a little over six days since the 'incident' had happened. Melony would slowly get back to normal, regain her physical strength, and return to her regular medication routine. The doctors agreed she would best do this at home. With the help of a therapist her nightmares should become less frequent, too. She might eventually take to closing her bedroom door at night, again. But for a while, she might wake in the middle of the night and crawl into bed with Ralph. An action he would never question or discourage. She would stop when she was ready.

Although Driscoll had been killed, his sister hadn't been caught yet, which meant that she was still out there somewhere. Ralph didn't think she posed a threat, on her own, but it still bothered him. Because of that, he knew he would have to double his efforts in protecting his family. He hoped that Emily would be arrested soon and put behind bars. He had hired Frank to do some checking to see if he could locate her. 'It will all work out for the better, sooner than later,' he said to himself as the thump-thump of Andrew's music came from his room, upstairs.

Ralph felt a tug on his sleeve. Looking over, he saw Melony standing beside the chair.

"Dad, will you read with me?"

Ralph motioned for Melony to get up on his lap. "Sure, why don't you read and I'll help you if you need it."

"Okay."

"What do you have tonight?" he asked, picking up the book she placed in his lap. "'Oscar and Boo.' That's a great book. One of your favorites, as I recall."

"Yes it is. I especially like Oscar."

"That's the cat, right?"

"No, Daddy. It's the spider. You know that," she said with a chuckle.

"Oh! Right. My mistake, Sweetie."

Melony read while Ralph listened and helped her along. When they finished, she asked, "Can we read one more?"

"Sorry, Dear. It's almost eight and you have to get ready for bed. Go up and I'll join you in a bit. And don't forget to brush your teeth."

"But Dad..." she started to protest, but stopped when Ralph gave her a stern look.

Melony headed upstairs. Ralph put away the book, checked all the locks, and headed up after her. He stopped by Andrew's room and opened the door a crack. The lights were on and his son lay awkwardly across the bed, still dressed, sound asleep. Ralph shut off the lights and stereo with a smile and closed the door. He went to Melony's room. "All set for bed?"

"Yeah, I guess so," she said with a half-pout.

Ralph tucked her in bed and gave her a kiss. "Remember, tomorrow we have a lot to do."

"Do I have to go?" she whined.

"You know you do. I've neglected it far too long."

"But, I'm a little scared."

"Don't worry. It'll be fine. I promise."

Just then Frisket brushed passed Ralph, hopped up on the bed, and settled in next to Melony. Ralph wasn't overjoyed with the dog sleeping in the bed, but it might help keep Melony calm, so he figured there was no harm in it. He turned to leave the room.

"You sure it will be okay?" Melony asked.

"Yes, I am. Remember what I told you."

"Don't be a menace to your dentist. They only want to make you smile pretty," she recited.

"Goodnight, Sweetheart."

"Goodnight, Dad."

THE END